Cowboys in Charge

Starla Kaye

ISBN 978-1-936556-14-4

Published 2015
Printed by Black Velvet Seductions Publishing
A division of Savage Publications

Visit us at:
www.blackvelvetseductions.com

Snowed in with Her Cowboy

"If you won't quit your job, at least take a couple of weeks off before Christmas." James walked into the bedroom carrying a cup of coffee for the woman he loved, the woman who frustrated the hell out of him lately. "There's no way you can keep the community commitments you've made and work forty plus hours a week. You're already dragging around, cranky."

Kelly peeked at him from the walk-in closet, a frown marring her pretty face. "I don't want to talk about this again. I'm not quitting."

"You don't even like working there," he reminded her. How many times had she complained over the last six months about her impossible-to-please boss, about the other women in the office who were always trying to backstab one another. She'd taken the job at Smithson's Architects because she didn't want her skills as an architect to fade away. He hadn't liked her going back to work, but he'd wanted her to be happy. She wasn't, though, which meant *they* weren't happy.

"Kelly, honey…" He hesitated because he didn't want to fight with her, especially before she went into Kansas City for another long day of work.

"Don't 'Kelly, honey,' me!" She stepped back into the closet. "We are *not* discussing this again! I'm not doing this to trample on your ego, cowboy. This isn't about you. It's about me."

After three years of marriage, he had a pretty good handle on his wife. She liked her independence and he gave her as much as possible. She spoke her mind without much thought first, which he also tolerated for the most part. She was easily twice as smart as him in many ways, which he admired. Her biggest flaw was once she made a decision, she stuck to it, even if that decision proved to be a bad one. Like this job. He was tired of watching her come home exhausted from the tension of a frustrating day at the office. He worried about her on the hour drive back to the ranch.

"You're wrong." He set the steaming cup of coffee on the dresser next to the door. "*This* is about *both* of us. You're my wife, dammit. It's my job to watch out for you, to step in when you're—"

"Watch it, macho boy!" She stormed out of the closet and tossed a skirt and blouse on the rumpled bed. Her brown eyes sparked with fire as she faced him. "I don't have time for you to go all Man in Charge on me this morning. I still need to take a shower and get dressed."

He curled his hands into fists at his sides. *She's tired. She's stressed. But, damn, so am I!* "Watch yourself. You're pushing this old boy right to his limits."

Her eyes continued to flash with irritation, her posture rigid. Then slowly she seemed to go limp. Her lower lip quivered. Tears glimmered in those weary eyes. All of the spit and fire went right out of her. "James," she whispered.

What the hell? Her sudden change surprised him as much as it worried him. He moved in front of her, his irritation gone. He wrapped his arms around her and clutched her to him. He could stand a lot of rough things in life, but the sight of his woman in tears gut punched him. Tears after he spanked her for one reason or another was different, those he expected and understood. For any other reason, though, they unmanned him, made him feel helpless.

"Baby, I'm sorry." He stroked her bare back, smoothed his hand over the wavy mass of long dark hair. Its silkiness, its sweet scent always got to him. But not anymore than the feel of her much smaller body in only lacy bra and panties did. His erection beneath his jeans immediately pressed between them. "It'll be okay. I'll make it okay." How, he didn't know.

She snuggled even closer, trembling. "I don't deserve you."

These highs and lows in her mood, her tiredness, her lack of appetite suddenly reminded him of something his brother-in-law had once said about James' sister. *"A pregnant woman can really try a man's patience sometimes."* His heart pounded and he fought to keep his excitement under control. He'd wanted this for so damn long. "You're pregnant, aren't you?" he asked quietly.

She stiffened. "What?" She shoved him away. Her plump breasts heaved in anger. "Of course I'm *not* pregnant! Why would you even think that?"

While disappointment crawled through him, she stomped toward the dresser and jerked out a slip. She tossed it on the bed beside her clothes. "I don't want kids right now. Maybe never. We've talked about this."

They had, before they got married and many times since then. She was great with kids; she'd make a good mother. But her complicated family history kept her from wanting to have a child. He'd tried to be patient, and hoped she would change her mind. Again, discontent and hurt spread through him. His patience was wafer thin. She didn't like her job. If she stayed home she could try that quilting stuff she'd talked about wanting to do. Or she could… He didn't know what else, but anything had to be better than working where she did now. And if she stayed home, maybe she'd soften toward the idea of having kids.

Her face was pinched tightly as she met him eye to eye. "Get that thought out of your head right now." When he started to protest, she forged onward, "Don't even try to deny it. You still think having me run around here bare foot and pregnant is the answer to my problem. God, that's so chauvinistic!"

Now he stood rigidly, tired to death of her calling him that. "It's not wrong for me to want children with you. We'd make great parents."

"*You* might, but *I* won't." The words came out briskly, yet he heard the pain and the fear in her voice. She was afraid to take the chance.

He shoved a hand through his hair. He just didn't know how to get through to her about this subject. She *wasn't anything* like her pitifully selfish mother. No matter how many times he tried to tell her that, she resisted. They'd discussed this last week and she'd almost left him. He'd been biting his tongue and acting as understanding as he could since then. No way was he losing her, even if he had to give up the idea of having kids.

Frustration made him reckless. "You're PMSing, aren't you?" He groaned at his stupidity. *What an idiot.*

Her eyes narrowed. "Because I'm not the sweet, biddable little woman you think I should be?" She snorted. "So what is *your* excuse for the changes in your attitude lately? Grouchy one minute, walking away the next. All kissy face one minute, turning away the next. Maybe *you* are the one PMSing."

He drew in deep, steadying breaths. This was really not going well. He should have gone on out to do his chores instead of bringing her a cup of coffee. Coffee that had probably turned cold by now. His efforts to be patient with her and not force another argument were straining things between them. His wanting to be tender with her and not pushy when she didn't seem to want to pursue making love had also failed. *Enough!*

"We need to deal with this tension between us." He glanced at the bed.

"We are *not* having sex right now. Just forget that nonsense." She shifted toward the attached bathroom.

James grabbed her arm and spun her to face him. "No, we aren't making love right now." He purposely didn't say 'having sex' because that word choice irritated him. "But I'm going to take care of someone's attitude problem."

He tugged her with him to the bed, even as she attempted to dig in her heels on the rug. "This is happening, honey. Your resisting is only going to make it more unpleasant."

Kelly's heart pounded, her whole body thrummed in anticipation. Her husband was going to spank her.

She'd pushed him to the breaking point this time. How had this gotten so out of control? She hadn't meant to attack him. Her head hurt, her heart hurt. Everything in her life seemed to be wrong at the moment. Her job. Their marriage. It was Christmas time and she usually loved this part of the year. This year it was yet another burden to bear.

He sat down on the side of the bed and drew her to his side, jerking her from her musings. "This isn't necessary," she said and looked anxiously at him. The sad expression on his ruggedly handsome face made her feel even worse. She loved this man with all of her heart, and yet lately all she seemed to do was argue with him and cause him pain.

"I think it is." He was gentle but determined as he guided her over his muscled thighs. "It's been a while since I've burned your butt. Usually it calms you down. I'm hoping it will again."

Sadly, he was right. A spanking took her mind away from her tendency to blow an issue out of proportion, which she realized she was doing now. It gave her something else to think about.

Resigned to the situation, she wriggled forward until she could put her hands on the rug. Her bottom rested on his right leg; her mound pressed against his jeans, separated only by the thin panties. Even knowing what was about to happen, her body tingled with awareness, longing.

"I've got to work today. Can't you wait until tonight?" she asked without much hope of changing his mind. He never did once he'd decided to spank her.

One of his hands eased the panties off her buttocks and she tensed, getting her answer without him speaking it.

She would have to deal with a sore ass. It wasn't the first time she'd had to suffer a spanking before work and then spend the day squirming on her chair. Still, she would rather not have had to experience it again.

"Do you know why you're getting spanked?" He settled his left forearm over her back and lightly tapped one bare cheek with his other hand.

Her buttocks quivered, clenched at the touch. Yes, she knew why. No, she didn't want to explain it. Instead she grumbled, "I don't have time to drag this out." She could imagine his frown at her not responding properly. He liked to go through this whole *why* thing ad nauseum, be sure she understood what she'd done wrong. Once the discussion part was over he would remind her that he only disciplined her for her own good. Uh-huh. Then came the spanking.

She felt the tension in his body; heard his teeth grinding in annoyance. But she wasn't in the mood for his routine. "Just spank me like you think I need," she blustered.

The smack that landed sent her jerking forward, had the air gasping out of her. "Okay! I'm sorry!" she cried. "I know this isn't how you like to do this. But I have to get to work."

He was quiet for a few seconds and then he blew out a frustrated breath. He lifted his arm from her back. "All right, I guess this can wait until tonight."

Tonight? Dread this all day? No, thank you. "No, no, no," she protested, craning her head to look back at him. "I'm already here in position, ready to accept the spanking. I don't want to be thinking about it all day. Just do it."

A vein pulsed in his neck and his brow furrowed. "You're awful pushy this morning." He nodded. "We've done this a time or two before you went to work. Guess you'll be able to deal with a sore butt this time, too."

She wanted to go back to his offer of doing this later, but it was too late. There would be no change of plans now. Disgusted with having pushed him to this, she lowered her head as he held her in place again. She loved and respected him, trusted him. She'd agreed to this kind of marriage, with occasional discipline.

"Lie still and we'll get this chore taken care of right quick."

The "right quick" part wasn't necessarily a good thing. She braced herself and gritted her teeth, determined to take her spanking with as much grace as possible.

With wicked aim, he sent smack after smack down to her vulnerable bottom. There wasn't time to breathe between the swats or to do more than wriggle in discomfort. It didn't take long before he got her to the point of understanding—or so he called it. He burned her bottom until she couldn't lie still, until she couldn't keep stoically quiet. He took her right to the point where she swore between sobs, "I'll…I'll behave better! I promise! I promise!"

A minute later she stood in front of him, between his legs, holding her hot, stinging bottom. Yes, she would have a tough day ahead, but at least she didn't have to spend all day thinking about going over his knee tonight. She gently rubbed at the sting, which didn't really help.

His expression softened as he watched her, satisfied that he'd done what he'd thought necessary. He never apologized for spanking her, but she knew he didn't enjoy doing it.

He reached up to thumb away the tears still trickling down her face. "Are we okay?"

"I've got a burning ass, but…" She sniffled and gave him a wobbly smile. "But, yes, we're okay." She would be sore today, but she didn't feel as testy anymore.

* * * *

James stood by the fireplace and sadness moved over him. Where had the time gone this month? This year? Christmas was only a couple of days away. He and Kelly hadn't fought since the spanking. She'd settled down, but her normal Christmas vigor was missing.

He stared at the Christmas tree he'd cut down this morning and hauled back to the house with the help of his ranch foreman. Tom hadn't said a word as they'd put the tree up and then toted box after box of decorations down from the attic. This was the first year she hadn't picked out a tree and helped him with the hauling and the decorating.

It didn't feel right to do this alone but they needed a tree. He knew how busy she was, how stressed she'd been. If all he could do to help her was put up their tree, he was more than glad to do it.

He stepped back to study the tree that sat by the stone fireplace. Had he hung too many lights? Not enough? Had he put on the ornaments she liked best? This wasn't his expertise, but he wanted to do it right for her. He wanted to take at least one of the usual tasks she performed at Christmas time off of her shoulders.

She'd spent several evenings this past week baking cookies for the ranchers' party and another one helping wrap presents for the community party last weekend. Plus they'd gone caroling with their church group one night and gone to a couple of get-togethers with neighbors. Between those long nights she'd worked extra hours at her job and squeezed in some shopping, which he'd done very little of. He didn't want to disappoint her, but he hadn't known what she wanted this year. Usually she gave him all kinds of hints. This year she hadn't said a word, not left one note around for him to find.

The pine scent drifted around him, made him miss Kelly. They hadn't had another argument in days. She'd been calmer since then, as usually happened after he helped tone down the craziness in her behavior. But he'd been right about the PMSing thing, so they hadn't made love yet. Fact was, he worried about *them*. She hadn't said anything, but he felt an uncomfortable distance between them. He wasn't sure they *were okay*, even if she'd told him they were after he'd burned her sweet ass. He was concerned.

He glanced out the window overlooking the ranch yard and frowned. It had started snowing not long after she'd left for the city this morning. He'd spent most of the day worrying about her. She was a good driver, but you never knew what could happen driving in snow. What he should have done was go into the city and get her. She'd probably have been irritated with him. No "probably" to it, she'd have been pissed. How many times had she told him, "I can take care of myself"? For the most part, she could. Still, with this weather, this time was different.

His cellphone rang and he blinked back to the moment. He pulled it from the holder on his belt. Seeing her number, his heart pounded. "Are you all right?" he asked in a rush.

"Yes, but..." She hesitated and he thought he might have a stroke while he waited for her to continue.

"But what?" He strode out of the great room and headed for his coat in the entry area.

"I left work early. I would have been home by now, but I sort of slid off the side of the highway."

He froze, felt the blood draining from his face. *Oh, God.* "Are you hurt?" He mentally kicked himself for letting her leave this morning when he'd heard on the news that snow was headed their way.

"I'm fine. Just have a bruise on my forehead from where I hit my head on the steering wheel. No big deal." She drew in a breath and said warily, "A man stopped to help me back onto the road. But there was some damage to my car. My front bumper hit a big rock in the ditch. It's not too bad, though, I promise."

He punched *Speaker* and set his phone down on the hall table while he pulled his heavy coat on.

He didn't know exactly where he was going, but he needed to get to her. In his near-panicked state, he recalled what she'd just said, heard the worry in her voice. "I could care less about the damn car, Kelly. *You* are all that matters to me."

She gave a weak sob and he felt almost certain it was one of relief. The thought that she might think he would be angry with her hurt him. Nothing mattered more to him than her. Nothing. Had he not made that clear to her already? Well, he damn sure would.

"Are you on your way now?" Was she talking to him on her phone while driving in this snowstorm? He almost snapped at her about that, but caught himself. She was driving, but he had to let that go. She was determined to get home to him. It humbled him. "Pull over, honey. Tell me where you are. I'm coming for you."

She gave a quick sniff, and he knew she was trying to cover up that she was crying. "I'm only a few miles away. I...I can make it."

He felt panicked, wanted to insist she wait for him to come get her. But there had been more than stubbornness in her tone. She needed to do this, make her way home on her own. He pulled in a steadying breath. It would be as hard as hell, but he would let her do it. "I'll be watching for you."

Kelly had never in her life been as scared as when her Honda CRV went into a skid on a patch of ice. Thank God she'd been almost crawling along the highway, like all of the other cars. The SUV had spun in a slow circle and then slid down the side of the road, stopping at the bottom of the short ditch where she'd hit a good-sized boulder. Her heart was still racing. She'd been fortunate one of the other cars had pulled over and a kindly older man had helped her. He'd offered to follow her home, but she'd told him she could manage.

It was such a relief to finally turn onto the gravel road leading to the ranch. Tears streamed down her face. *Almost there.* James would be waiting for her, watching from the porch no doubt. She'd heard the anxiety in his voice and had known he wanted to come get her. He was always so determined to be the strong one, to take care of her.

Including spanking her when she got all snappy with him, or when she stubbornly went against him for whatever reason, or when she did something stupid. Like going to work when she'd heard on the early morning news about the snow coming and ignoring what the smart thing would have been to do: call in and say she wouldn't be in today. If he wanted to turn her over his knee, she'd go willingly. She'd been stupid, endangered herself, gotten her car damaged, and—worst of all—needlessly worried her husband.

She'd made some decisions in the last few days, hopefully good ones. She just hoped that she hadn't waited too long. If she lost him because of the horrible person she'd turned into lately... But he'd sounded so worried about her. He loved her. She would hold firmly to that belief and if necessary, do whatever she had to in order to make sure he still did. Her Christmas gifts to him this year were a bit out of the ordinary, but, hopefully, would be exactly what he wanted.

With a sigh and a silent prayer of thanksgiving, she turned into the ranch yard. Every light on the barn and other buildings and the house were on, making her feel welcome. The dark afternoon no longer seemed so depressing. And there on the porch, just as she'd suspected, stood James. Her big, sometimes gruff, cowboy. So much love filled her that she thought her heart just might burst with it. How had she ever been lucky enough to find him? Why he'd wanted her, stuck by her, still wanted her, amazed her. He didn't care about her past or the kind of horrible family she came from. None of that stuff mattered to him. How many times had he told her that? How many times had she been unable to believe him?

She pulled into the driveway and turned off the engine. She watched him stride down the porch steps and walk quickly toward her, oblivious to the foot of snow he tromped through. He focused on her, only her. Her stomach fluttered. Her pulse raced. All she needed for the rest of her life was this very special man.

He tugged the car door open and leaned inside to kiss her. She trembled as his big, cold hands cupped her face. She kissed him back, put her hands on his beard-roughened face. Everything she'd gone through on this horrible day was forgotten. She was home now. With James.

He inched back and then before she knew what he was going to do, he scooped her up and out of the car. It wasn't the first time he'd carried her, but it was the most precious time. The tender look in his eyes, the sheen of tears he'd held back because of her, touched her to the depth of her soul.

As he nudged the car door shut with his hip, she said quietly, "I love you. I know I don't say that very often, but I do. I love you."

He tromped back through the snow, up the steps, and into the house. He held her close and didn't seem to care at all that snow was melting off his boots onto the tiled floor. "You don't have to say the words, honey, I know."

"But you deserve the words," she protested, feeling guilty. She rarely said *love*, hadn't trusted in the emotion. Until James.

"Actions show what you feel for me." He slowly let her down. His gaze stayed locked with hers. "You turned this old house into a home, filled it with loving touches. Photos of my family, of you and me, on the mantle." He grinned crookedly. "You bake me snickerdoodle cookies because I have a sweet tooth. You watch old Westerns with me, when I know you really don't like them."

He'd never told her these things meant anything to him, not that she did any of that to be praised. But she felt uncomfortable, knowing he'd done so much more for her from the moment they'd met. Needing a second to compose herself, she turned toward the great room. Then she really lost it.

"Oh, James," she gasped, gaping at the decorated tree. She blinked rapidly to keep the tears at bay. "You put up a tree for me."

"For *us*. Having a Christmas tree is something that means a lot to both of us."

She heard the gentleness in his voice. He was right. They'd enjoyed spending a cold day picking out the perfect tree each of the last two years. They teased each other over how to hang the lights just right. They fought—playfully—over who would put the angel on top of the tree. And hanging the decorations from his family and ones they had bought together meant a lot to her…to both of them. But he'd done it all by himself this year. For her.

Christmas was two days away and usually they exchanged their presents on Christmas Eve. But she couldn't wait that long. Although she was nervous, she needed to give him her gifts now. At least some of them.

Heart pounding, she looked up at him. "Wait for me by the tree. Please. I have something I want to give you and I can't wait for tomorrow."

"But…" He stopped protesting when she went up on tiptoes and kissed him silent.

She turned and jerked off her coat, thrusting it into his hands. Then she raced to the spare bedroom.

All James wanted to do was take Kelly to their bedroom and make love to her, over and over, and over some more. He'd been so damn worried about her. He could have lost her and he couldn't imagine his life without her in it.

He'd watched her smiling uncertainly at him before she hurried up the stairs. Instinct warned him something important was about to happen. Something far more than just exchanging gifts early.

Damn! Gifts! He still hadn't wrapped the few presents he'd gotten her. What the hell did he do now? No way was he going to accept something from her without giving something in return. The stupidest idea flashed into his head. Well, he was a man. Sometimes men got really dumb, desperate ideas.

Kelly carried three small wrapped gifts down the stairs. Would he think these ridiculous? She'd come up with this idea yesterday. What would he say? She almost turned around to go back and grab the other "real" presents she'd gotten him.

But the sound of soft Christmas music playing snagged her attention. Her favorite songs. Then she noticed that James had turned off all the lights in the lower part of the house except for the Christmas lights.

Curious and warmed by his thoughtfulness, she walked slowly closer. At first she didn't spot him, since she was taking in the wonder of the beautifully decorated tree. Then he quietly coughed to draw her attention. She froze, stunned. And then laughed for the first time in far too long. *Her precious, precious cowboy.*

"Got to admit that *wasn't* the reaction I was hoping for," he mumbled. He hastily reached for one of the throw pillows he'd put on the floor near him and held it across his lower body.

Struggling to stop giggling, to quit grinning like a fool, she hurried to him. She dropped down on her knees beside her very naked, very tempting husband. She set her gifts to the side and pulled the pillow off him. His long, thick cock adorned with a red bow from the tree danced toward her. She gently took hold of it and smiled at his quiet groan of pleasure.

"Best gift ever." She stroked the velvety softness of the steel-like rod. "I plan to spend a long time enjoying it later tonight."

She glanced warily at the presents next to her. "I…I hope you like my gifts as much."

James found it almost impossible to concentrate on anything but the way Kelly's hand held his dick. It felt so good. Hell, more than good. He wanted to tumble her to the floor and spend hours and hours showing her how much he loved her. But he could tell she was nervous, concerned about her gifts for him. When she released him to reach for the small boxes, he fought back a groan of complaint.

He shifted up into a sitting position and took the first red-wrapped present from her shaking hands. He waited for her to say something. When she didn't, he ripped off the paper. Lifting the top off the box, he pulled out a piece of paper carefully folded inside. *I respectfully give my notice. December 23 will be my last day.* There was more, clearly this was a copy of her letter of resignation to her boss.

He was so damn happy he could have done one of those crazy happy dances.

"Stupid, huh?" She anxiously twisted her hands in her lap.

The job had been important to her so he held his happiness in check. "Are you sure about this? I don't want to pressure you, not really."

Her chin jutted up. "It's what *I* want. Are you okay with it, though? I know the extra money is nice."

"Hell, yes, I'm okay!" He started to reach for her, but she thrust a second present at him.

He wanted to hug her…and so much more. Instead he opened the long, slender box, thinking it looked like a tie box, although he never wore ties. When he lifted the lid off the box, he blinked twice at the foot and a half long riding crop with a heart-shaped top.

As he held it up curiously, he noted his wife's pink cheeks. "A crop? Really?" He damn sure would never have expected something like this. He hadn't known she even knew about such things. Clearly there were a lot of things he didn't know about his wife.

She pursed her lips for a second and then said primly, "It's supposed to deliver a 'sweet surprise' for when I've been 'very, very good.' At least that's what the salesclerk told me."

Hmm, where exactly had she gone shopping? Interesting. He raised an eyebrow in challenge. "I bet it can deliver a stinging smack, too, when you've been very, very bad."

She started to jerk it out of his hands, but he moved it out of her reach, grinning. "We'll save it for those 'very good' times."

While she calmed, stopped looking so irritated, he nodded at her final wrapped package.

Without commenting any further about the crop, she handed him the last gift. She worried her lower lip and he sensed *this* one meant the most to her. He tore the paper away slowly, uncertain. He sure as hell hoped he wouldn't disappoint her with his reaction to whatever this was.

Seeming impatient, she grabbed the box and yanked off the lid. She took the shredded pieces of paper out and thrust them at him. Then she closed her eyes and waited.

He glanced at a couple pieces before he finally realized what he held. He struggled to speak. "The prescription renewal for The Pill. You tore it up? Why?" He prayed he understood. He could barely contain his need to hug her to him.

Those beautiful, loving eyes of hers opened and she said timidly, "It's time we had a baby."

He didn't care that he felt moisture on his face. This was a precious moment, one he'd thought might never happen. He held out his arms and she crawled onto his lap. "Best Christmas ever."

She leaned back, thumbed away the tears from his cheeks. "No. The best Christmas ever was when we met at that party four years ago."

He glanced out the window, noticed that the snow was falling even heavier now. He didn't mind it at all. "Looks like we're going to be snowed in here for a spell, honey."

"Works for me." She cuddled closer.

Worked for him, too.

Too Much Red at Christmas Time

I will not buy this for Trent. I will not get him one more present. I won't. I mean it. I won't.

Lizzie Morgan heaved a sigh so deep it came up from her toes. She stood in the men's area of Patterson's Department Store, Christmas music playing overhead, last minute shoppers milled around as they searched for gifts they should have bought before the stock was so picked over. She didn't need to be here, but she had this bizarre addiction to Christmas gift shopping. She couldn't stop.

*But you **need** to stop. Now. Forget these gloves. Just walk away.*

She glanced at her best friend Suzy for support in her decision. "I shouldn't buy these. Right?"

Suzy shook her head, chin-length blonde hair shining under the fluorescent lighting. "Absolutely not. Trent warned you not to charge anything else. His stern command when we left your house is still ringing in my ears." Her forehead pinched and she sighed in resignation. "But you're going to buy those gloves anyway."

"They'll keep his hands nice and toasty this winter." Lizzie studied the fine leather gloves with rabbit fur lining. She reached onto the counter and ran her fingers over the inside of one glove. "It's so soft."

"They're not gloves for doing ranch work and that's all he does." Suzy studied the gloves, frowned. "Trent won't appreciate this gift nearly as much as you do." Ever the logical, responsible one in their friendship, she attempted to pull the gloves away.

Stubborn to the core especially about something she wanted to buy, Lizzie refused to let go of the gloves. "I'm getting them." A part of her knew her friend was right. But a fluttery feeling in her stomach at not making this purchase couldn't be ignored. It didn't matter that she liked the gloves far more than he probably ever would. She rubbed a finger along the inside again and almost purred. The lining was so soft, irresistible. She'd like to have gloves like these.

"I can see how much they appeal to you," Suzy said and nodded toward the women's section of the department store. "Why don't you just buy some similar ones for yourself? Forget these."

Lizzie jutted out her chin at the challenge. "Maybe he'll get me some for Christmas. I've already hinted at least a hundred times about them."

She rolled the comment around in her head. He was such a man. He wouldn't remember the hints…about any of the things she'd mentioned in the last month. He could remember every teeny tiny item the ranch needed, but something she wanted? Nope. She'd probably get another scarf he found somewhere, something that didn't require knowing her size. And he'd give her a box with a couple of gift cards. He'd smile as he told her it was best this way.

Depression weighed her down. Just once she'd like to get something he took more than two seconds to pick out for her. She didn't care what color it was, what size it was. She just wanted to feel as important to him as his stupid ranch. She knew it was childish. She knew he loved her…but still…

"I'm getting these for Trent and that's final." She was buying the gloves for him because he wouldn't buy them for her. Twisted logic, maybe. If he would just buy gifts that she actually hinted about, actually wanted, maybe she wouldn't be this insistent. And if he didn't get her gloves for Christmas, she'd go buy them herself.

She picked the gloves up and marched with her other items toward the line at the check-out counter. It was only a week before Christmas and the lines were long. Many of the women in line wore the harried look of holiday shoppers who wished they had started shopping months ago. One scratched things off a crumpled list in her hand. Another studied a paper, worrying her lip in distress, and then mumbled something very un-holiday like.

Lizzie was thankful she didn't have their problems. She'd started buying gifts for her husband and his ranch hands during the summer. She was done with her Christmas shopping but she just couldn't seem to stop shopping. There were so many bargains, so many additional items that called to her. Like these gloves Trent didn't need.

Suzy walked up behind her and whispered grimly, "You are going to be in so much trouble when he sees all these gifts." She glanced at the knitted stocking cap, the Christmas boxers, and the shower radio Lizzie also carried. "Trent won't use any of these things. Set them aside." She sighed. "You really should take some of the other gifts you bought today back, too."

"No." Again, her friend was right. She should return maybe a dozen of the extra shirts, belts, and socks she'd bought the men in the last week. What she'd bought two months ago would be more than enough. Except that she didn't believe in returning anything, which was another issue she and her husband disagreed on. It was embarrassing, always made her feel like a fool.

"What did he tell you last month when the credit card statement came?" Suzy prodded. "He's a man of his word, Lizzie."

She was getting tired of her friend trying to act as her conscience, forcing her to remember that Trent had little tolerance for her going against agreements they'd made with one another. In particular about keeping to a budget. *Money is tight, Lizzie, we need to watch every cent we spend.* His words played through her thoughts. She knew things had gotten tighter this last year, but she thought he was being overly cautious too much of the time. *Why can't you understand how important it is to stick to the budget? Am I going to have to take away your credit card?* Lately she'd even had nightmares about the budget, about the pressure of sticking to it.

Sometimes he could be such a Scrooge. Once she'd shouted it at Trent and then promptly gotten her bottom burned. Name calling was *not* tolerated. Scrooge. Scrooge. Scrooge!

The line inched slowly forward and she started sweating beneath her knee-length leather coat, and not from heat. No, she started thinking about Trent's warning before they'd left the ranch. About how angry he'd been last month when she'd reached the limit on their credit card. He'd nearly had a stroke, but he'd paid it off, taking money from their savings. He'd also lectured her royally about the problem of her being reckless with their money. Of course she'd snapped back at him that she *didn't* have a problem. He was just being a tightwad, Scrooge. The subject had remained a sore point between them ever since.

She glanced at the gloves, the boxers, the radio, the stocking cap, and the bottles of men's cologne for each of the six ranch hands. Okay, maybe Trent didn't need a few of those items. Maybe the men didn't normally wear cologne. But they could.

She tensed, her stomach contracting to a tight ball. She'd lost some of the receipts lately, from store purchases and online ones as well. Just how much *had* she spent? Nausea threatened.

"Next in line," the sales clerk called out, pulling her from her anxious thoughts.

Suzy nudged her forward. "You can still change your mind." She planted her hand on the expensive gloves. "Save yourself some grief later." *Pain too*, was implied. One of the many things they had in common was being married to men who believed in spanking.

Lizzie shoved her friend's hand away and glowered at her. "Everything will be fine. I'm buying these." Yet, even as she made the assertion, she tingled all over, and not in eager anticipation. There was a very good chance she'd spend Christmas afternoon or the next day— maybe both—standing a lot. But such was her life with a husband who had an almost rigid set of rules and a hard hand to make her pay when she went against them. Good thing she loved the old poop head.

* * * *

It had been a hell of a long day. Trent had dealt with one problem after another ever since he had walked into the bunkhouse at dawn and found two of his men sick with the flu. He supposed it would pass around to everyone on the ranch in the next week or so. Perfect. Right at Christmas time with so much to do to get ready for snow that would be coming before long, with family and friend get-togethers that he was too tired to even think of attending—but would anyway.

Flu. Damn, damn, damn. Maybe he and Lizzie wouldn't get it since he'd insisted both of them get flu shots last month. He never liked getting sick and what it did to his over-burdened life. He would hate it even more if it interfered with his plans for him and his wife. For once in over six years of marriage, he'd put some real thought into a Christmas gift for her. Actually, it was for both of them. His surprise was costing him—them—a good chunk of money, which made him nervous. But for once he was tightly reining in the Scrooge side of him. When she'd called him a scrooge and a tightwad during a recent argument about money, he'd suddenly wondered if maybe he did have that tendency. At least with her.

He glanced at her as she got up from the table. He loved her and wanted her to have everything she wanted, but recently it was getting damn hard to afford. He was getting concerned about all her shopping trips into town with Suzy.

He swallowed the last bite of roast beef, so full he really needed to loosen the top button on his jeans. His sweet little wife could be one fine cook when she put her mind to it. Usually when she wanted to get on his good side. But she *wasn't* on his good side and she knew it.

He pushed his chair back from the dinner table and wished he could simply go watch TV or even read some more of the book he'd started last week. But he had an unpleasant chore to take care of first. Lizzie had gotten a speeding ticket coming back from Hays this afternoon. They'd talked before about her tendency to have a heavy foot on the gas pedal. This was her second ticket in three months. The worst of it was that she hadn't intended to tell him about this one. He only knew about it because he'd noticed it sticking out of her purse that she'd left on the counter when she'd carried some bags up to the spare bedroom. He knew she was storing the Christmas gifts in there and he was honestly afraid to go in there and see all that she'd bought.

"You go ahead and relax, honey," Lizzie said, scurrying away from the table with her hands full of dishes. She didn't even look in his direction.

"I will, in a few minutes." He watched her stiffen at the grimness in his tone. She should feel uneasy because she knew how much trouble she was in.

She sucked in a breath and set the dishes on the counter over the dishwasher. Still she didn't glance back at him. "I really should go to the courthouse and protest the ticket. I'm sure I was only going maybe five miles over the limit."

He knew her better than that. He also knew she always did her best to skirt around something she'd done wrong. Like getting another well-deserved ticket. Not taking responsibility for her actions was one of her bad habits they were working on by mutual agreement.

"Let's not play this game tonight, Elizabeth." She would understand that by using her given name he was upset with her and wasn't going to simply back down. The matter would be settled right now, at least as far as between them. She would have to pay the fine later.

Warily she turned to face him, her face a little pale, lines of tension bracketing her mouth. "You're tired. I'm tired. Can't we just..." She stopped when he shook his head.

"Get your sweet ass over here. Now." Disciplining her was always difficult. He believed in domestic discipline and it seemed to be helping her with breaking some bad habits, but he didn't enjoy it. Right now he'd rather have nearly-kill-him, wild sex with her. But she needed more from him at times, like a well-applied hand to her pretty butt.

She hesitated, clearly not interested in obeying. No big surprise there. She took a sound spanking, but she didn't like the hours of dealing with a sore bottom afterward.

"Elizabeth."

"Oh fine," she snapped and blew out an exasperated breath. She stomped over to him. Her eyes sparked with irritation. "I really don't want to do this." And yet she'd come to him.

When she stood in front of him, expression pinched in annoyance, he reached out to unfasten her jeans. She remained perfectly still because it was expected of her. His fingers brushed her soft skin and he fought back instant desire. Her stomach quivered and he heard her quick intake of breath. She was affected, too. He ignored her reaction as well.

"You should have thought about that before you put the gas pedal to the floorboard." He concentrated on pulling down the zipper, on what he was doing and why. It wasn't easy, though.

"I did no such thing!" she objected, although her cheeks turned pink and she didn't meet his eyes.

She'd always been a terrible liar. He pushed the jeans down to mid-thigh. The sight of her creamy legs had his body tightening and he struggled to focus on his task. He braced himself for tugging down her bikini panties and seeing the curly dark hair covering the place he ached to be inside of.

It took him a second before he could get past that. He swallowed hard. "The ticket said you were going *twenty* miles over the speed limit. *Not five.*"

She opened her mouth to protest, but his dark look had her saying meekly, "His meter thing might be wrong."

He arched an eyebrow, telling her he wasn't buying the excuse. As her shoulders slumped, he pulled her to his side and then over his lap. He waited as she wriggled into position, but watching her do so had him grinding his teeth. Even through the thick denim, he felt every squirm of her delectable body. There were times when he suffered almost as much during these spankings as she did. Almost.

Her hands flattened on the tile and her long dark hair fell around her face. Still fighting down an erection, he looked wearily at the butt he was about to heat up. It was such a shame to spank her and send her to bed. Even if he was tired tonight, he would rather have spent their time together now in a much different way. A thought that made his situation worse and had him trying to think of anything but sinking deep inside her. But even listing off the chores to do tomorrow, the supplies he needed to get, did little to stop his body's reaction to his wife.

"Get it over with already," she grouched, jerking him back to the moment. She was always pissy when she was about to get spanked.

Relieved and irritated at the same time, he swatted her clenched cheeks hard enough to make her jerk her head up.

"No warm up?" she complained on a hiss.

His hand landed equally hard a second time. "No. Elizabeth Morgan, you have far too much attitude today. But I'm fixing to take care of that problem."

"Then do it." She settled down again, muttering, "You know I hate dragging this out."

"More attitude? Really?" He could be as obstinate as she could be snippy. He held still, his hand raised high for another smack. "You're being far pushier than normal. What's that about?"

She refused to answer him. She was always out of sorts when he was punishing her. But this was different. Something else was going on with her. Something he would find out about later and have to deal with. He knew it gut deep. Lizzie could really test him at times. But he loved her, bad habits, crankiness, occasional disobedience and all.

Lizzie stared at the floor, feeling almost cross-eyed as she waited for her husband to get on with the spanking. *Attitude.* Yes, she wasn't the least bit happy with the situation. It was bad enough that she'd bought all of those extra presents that he would be seriously upset about later. But she'd been stupid enough to push the speed limit, again.

"Are you ready?" he asked, his legs stiffening beneath her as he prepared himself.

She rolled her eyes, huffed in disgust as she realized he couldn't see her response. "If I said *no?*"

"What do you think?"

"That you would know I was stalling. That you are going to burn my butt anyway." She pulled in a breath and waited for him to get down to business.

He didn't let her down. The man knew how to give a proper spanking. He was expert at tenderizing every inch of her poor bottom, and then doing it some more. Wriggling all over his lap, kicking up her legs, arching her back…none of it waylaid him from his task. And she certainly got her exercise in during a firm butt busting lesson.

She was biting down the need to cry out in pure stubbornness when he sent the hardest smack yet to her sit spot. That did it. She yelped, "Ohhh, gawd!"

He added one lighter smack for good measure. "Okay, we're done here," he sounded relieved.

She collapsed in misery and let the tears slide down her cheeks. Well and truly spanked. Again. She really needed to stop getting into trouble with him.

After another few seconds, she sucked in a steadying breath and eased off his lap. Her bottom was on fire and she desperately wanted to reach back and try to smooth away the sting. Something which never really worked. Instead, she stood in front of him, blinking away tears, and fisting her hands at her sides. She wanted to flee to their bedroom and pout about what had happened. But she couldn't until he told her it was okay to do so.

He studied her, searching her eyes for an admission of some kind. He suspected she had more to tell him. She did, but wasn't ready to get into that right now. Although it would probably mean she'd suffer another spanking later.

"Is there something else you want to tell me, sweetheart?" he prodded, his brow creased in concern.

"Um, no."

He sighed heavily, looking disgusted. Even as annoyed as he was, he still had trouble keeping his gaze above where her jeans rested low on her legs. She felt him staring at the beads of moisture on her bush. Her bottom might hurt, but she still got aroused being half-dressed and close to him. And she'd felt his erection pressing against her, could still see it. But he didn't believe in mixing discipline with pleasure.

She might ache for having him pound into her in his wonderfully hot cowboy way, but she would rather wait a while. He liked her to have time to come to terms with having been spanked. In truth, she got past that part really quick. She used his staying-away-from-her time to get ready for the make-up sex.

"Are you sure?" he asked, but his expression told her he already knew her answer.

"Not now," she mumbled.

"Shit. That definitely means there's more." His shoulders slumped and he shook his head. "Go to bed."

She experienced a second's hesitation. Should she just get everything out there? Take another spanking now and be done with it? No.

Resigned, she fell back onto their standard procedure. She carefully pulled her clothes back into place, wincing, and hurried from the room. It looked like cleaning up tonight was his chore. Not like it was the first time.

* * * *

Christmas Eve had finally arrived. Lizzie knew she should be wrapping the rest of the gifts and carting them downstairs. But as she stood in the middle of the spare bedroom staring at everything she'd piled onto the bed she couldn't work up the energy to do it. She'd really bought *that* much extra stuff? They had been to one neighbor or another's every night this last week. She'd cooked a ton of cookies, candies, and pies. She'd helped with wrapping gifts at the department store as part of a volunteer project. The list went on and on. Basically she was dead-dog tired.

A glance at her watch told her she had at least another four hours before Trent would end his workday. She already had beef stew in the Crockpot and fresh, homemade bread cooling on the counter. What would it hurt if she took a quick nap? An hour would surely revive her enough to finish the last of the wrapping chore.

She carefully shut the door and walked on weary legs toward their bedroom. A shiver of unease snaked up her spine. Trent had already groaned and grumbled this morning when he'd seen the additional presents she'd shoved under the tree yesterday. She wasn't sure she could even get any more under there. Maybe she should just forget these others. She could stash them away for next year. But she didn't really like that idea.

Dragging herself to the big bed, she dropped onto it. She glanced at the clock on her nightstand. Okay, an hour. She'd not take longer than that.

* * * *

Trent decided to call it a day earlier than he'd planned to. All of these hard days and partying nights were getting to him. He was only thirty-two but some days he felt like he was sixty. He walked into the mudroom next to the kitchen. Shoving his boots off, he drew in the scent of stew. His stomach rumbled. He breathed in deeper. Fresh bread, too. One of his favorite smells. His Lizzie had outdone herself today.

He hung his coat on a wall peg and headed into the kitchen, grinning, eager to see his wife. He was as hungry for her as he was for the stew. They'd barely done more than kiss in days, since that last discussion about her spending problem and the speeding ticket. Both still bothered him. Why couldn't he get through to her?

Frustrated, he forced those thoughts aside for now. Instead he focused on that sexy little red corset and matching panties he'd boldly ordered online a while back. He'd thought about how she'd look in them from the second the package arrived. *Damn hot.* Exactly how she'd look. Christmas red. Her best color. 'Course he didn't plan on her wearing them for all that long a time.

His dick pressed at the front of his jeans. That vision of her wearing the sexy red number was driving him crazy. Maybe he'd give her this particular gift tonight instead of waiting for tomorrow morning. They could have some extra fun tonight. That sounded like a hell of an idea.

Where is she? Anxious to get started with that plan, he went looking for her.

She wasn't in the great room, but the heavily decorated tree was…with a mountain of wrapped gifts both under and beside it. He gritted his teeth, felt his stomach contract like a fist. She'd gone overboard again. Even after they'd had a serious discussion about the matter in early November. He didn't even want to think about how much money she'd spent on all of these things.

He didn't feel quite as enthusiastic to find her now, but he walked up the stairs. As he neared their bedroom, he heard her light snores and smiled, amused. *I don't snore!* How many times had she told him that? He should record it sometime and play it back for her. Except that would just tick her off.

The door to the spare bedroom was closed as he started by it. He stopped, a sinking feeling hitting him. There couldn't be *more* gifts still in there. Of course not. Yet he drew in an anxious breath and turned the doorknob. His gaze landed on the bed. *Shit!*

Anger curled through him, made him jerk the door closed again with a loud slam that shook the walls. *Damn, damn, damn!*

He strode to their bedroom, chest pounding. All thoughts of giving his wife that sexy outfit fled. But she'd be wearing red tonight… on her ass. He couldn't tolerate this senseless spending any longer. She would listen to him this time, at least she'd get his message in a memorable way.

She must have heard the door slam because she sat up on the bed when he entered the room, blinking away the fuzziness of sleep. When she spotted him and his no doubt sour expression, she said warily, "You're upset with me. Why now?"

Trent headed straight for the walk-in closet, counting to ten, twenty, and fifty as he went. He stood inside and waited until his breathing had settled. "Didn't we talk just yesterday about all the presents under the tree? I told you there were too many. And you swore that was all of them. Remember that discussion?"

She remained quiet. He bunched his fists but didn't move. "Well?" he challenged.

"Yes," she assured, her voice little more than a whisper.

He closed his eyes and sucked in a settling breath. He'd heard the guilt underlying her simple answer. No doubt she realized from the loud door slamming what he'd just seen. And she knew what she faced now. Dammit, this was Christmas Eve!

Glancing at the special red leather paddle hanging beside the door, he clenched his jaw. He didn't want to do this. Yet he couldn't let the problem fester between them. That wasn't their way. It had to be faced and dealt with.

He walked back into the bedroom carrying the paddle used for more serious "discussions." It felt wrong in his hand, but necessary.

Her pretty eyes widened, glistened with tears. "Supper is ready," she said instead of an actual protest.

"It smells good, too, but it'll wait." He touched the paddle to the side of his leg and she watched the movement, dread in her eyes. "We don't even need to talk about the problem this time, do we? You know what it is."

She shook her head. "No." She swallowed hard, barely breathing.

He moved to the side of the bed. "Your choice: over my knee or over the pillows."

"Pillows." She couldn't meet his eyes.

He almost tossed the paddle aside, almost decided to let her act of misbehavior go this time. But, damn, this was important. And she expected to pay for what she'd done by taking another spanking. He couldn't ignore this matter.

"Shove those jeans down, too." While she waited, he stacked two pillows in the middle of the bed. He concentrated on getting them just right and not on how she trembled nearby.

She glanced at him and then climbed on the bed behind the pillows. Her face flamed as she wiggled her jeans down before stretching over the pile. His cock responded instantly at the sight of her. His body desperately wanted to climb up there behind her, bend her over, and drive into her. It would be wild, hard, and fast.

Somehow he managed to force that longing aside and grit out, "Shift your legs apart a bit."

He preferred this position when he paddled her, but it was torture for him. Seeing those soft folds, that swollen clit, the way her ass quivered...

"I know you don't believe me, but I'm sorry," she said quietly, lowering her head to the mattress. "Sorry I keep disappointing you."

Her remorse tugged at him. But they'd talked about this too many times already. He'd spanked her for similar instances of overspending. It couldn't keep happening.

He sent the first swat across both cheeks. They sunk in beneath the paddle and a line of red showed when he lifted it. "This is serious, Elizabeth." He swatted her two more times. "Why can't you understand that?"

She gasped. Her fingers curled around the comforter. "I mean to follow what we agreed to. I just... I just..."

The paddle expressed his frustration several more times causing her to yelp with each blow. Her butt was already getting red and he felt the heat rising off of it. He didn't like doing this, but whenever he spanked her for something, she didn't repeat the misbehavior for a long time. He wished she never did.

He held the paddle against where it had last fallen as she caught her breath. "I don't know how to make this clear to you. You tell me one thing—promise me—and then go out shopping again. Like we hadn't even discussed the subject."

"I know it's wrong," she whimpered, tightening her fingers even more on the comforter, knowing there was more to come.

He considered stopping, debated it until she looked back at him expectantly. He focused on the unpleasant task and sent another smack down, but not as hard. He didn't want to really hurt her.

She lowered her head, sobbed, "I'm so sorry." She hiccupped. "I don't even like going shopping that much. But I...I just have to."

She just had to? She felt compelled to shop? Her emotions were driving her to do this? He had a bad feeling about this now. Something he'd read somewhere.

"Answer me honestly, sweetheart. Do you have stashes of things you've bought? Besides these Christmas gifts? Things you didn't want me to know about?" He waited uneasily for her answer.

It took her a few seconds before she bobbed her head. "Yes," she whispered. "I'm so sorry."

His gut tightened as he recognized real remorse, her embarrassed guilt. This wasn't like other acts of disobedience. This was something else.

Time for disciplining her was done. She'd paid enough for these recent purchases. They needed to talk about this matter. He walked across the room and set the paddle on the dresser. He tried to figure out how to broach the subject. She had a problem. This was more than just a way of her rebelling against anything they'd agreed to.

Uncertain and worried, he eased onto the bed next to the woman he loved with all of his heart. He wouldn't make her deal with this problem alone. "Come here, sweetheart."

She hadn't moved out of position and looked at him in confusion, blinking away tears. "You're finished? Already?"

He grimaced as he saw how red her ass was, at knowing how much pain she suffered. A spanking always hurt. A paddling, even a short one, seriously stung. And he'd given her a number of swats where he'd barely held his strength back. When she deserved discipline, he could live with her temporary pain. But now... now he felt guilty.

"Yes, I'm done paddling you." He gave her a tender look. "Come here, sweetheart. I need to hold you." How would she take what he had to say?

She didn't hesitate to shift off the pillows and to snuggle against him. She trembled and made sure not to touch her tender butt to the mattress. He could barely hear her as she said, "I know I bought way too much for Christmas this year." She sniffled. "I just can't help myself. Suzy told me to stop. But I couldn't."

Trent held her to him, running his hand soothingly up and down her back. "I read an article recently about women who can't seem to stop shopping. Shopaholics. They buy things they don't need or really even want. They just can't help themselves."

She lifted her head to look at him. "Really? This is an addiction?" She hesitated and admitted sadly, "It's been getting worse since this summer. But I don't know why."

He gently touched her face. "It's a compulsion, but they don't seem to know for sure what causes it."

He considered something else he remembered hearing and guilt tore through him. "Some psychiatrists think the compulsive behavior is triggered by a need to feel special." He felt even worse as he added, "To combat loneliness."

His words played over again in his head. *Loneliness.* He knew then that a lot of the problem lay at his feet. He would own up to it and they'd figure this out together. He held her gaze as she looked up at him. "God, sweetheart, I did this to you."

Her pretty brow furrowed. "I'm the one who—"

"The one who needed me to be around more," he interrupted. He blew out a breath of frustration. "I've been so crazy busy with the ranch this year. I've all but ignored you. I'm so sorry, so very sorry."

He saw the truth in her eyes: he'd been right. He'd been too distant, too damn busy. But she gave him a wobbly smile. "I know how demanding the ranch can be." She hugged him back.

He took comfort in the fact that she had latched on to him almost as desperately as he had to her. "We'll get you help. We'll fix this. I promise."

She shook her head. "This isn't *your* fault. Well, maybe partially. I don't mind sharing the blame about this problem."

"Always. We need to share *all* of our problems. I love you, sweetheart, more than you can possibly know." He couldn't imagine life without her. "I swear to you that I'm going to stop being such an inconsiderate husband." He would never again let her think that she wasn't important to him.

Tears misted her eyes again. "So, does that mean you'll help me wrap those other presents you found?"

"You're pushing things, Lizzie. But I'll help you take them back."

She looked worried, anxious. "I can't! I..." She sucked in a breath. "Okay, maybe."

Trent knew he needed to learn a lot more about this compulsive need his wife suffered from. The panic he'd seen in her eyes just now warned him this might be difficult for both of them. But they'd get through it.

To distract her—him, too, he decided to admit to his big expenditure this year. He felt nervous for a second and then determined. "Actually, I spent a lot this year, too. I wanted to give you something special. Something to show you how much I love you. I know sometimes you think I ignore you or put you second to the ranch. But I don't mean to."

She leaned back, her eyes sparkling with delight. "What is it? Don't make me wait until tomorrow. Please."

He gave her a frown, certain his crooked smile ruined it. "Well, I have a few *small* presents under the tree, so I suppose..." The happiness on her beloved face was too much for him. He blurted out, "I got us tickets to Maui the second week in January. A week's stay in a fancy resort, too."

Tears streamed down her cheeks, but at his stricken look, she dashed them away. "It's perfect. You're perfect." Then she began shoving off her jeans. "Strip. Now."

He gaped at her.

She climbed off the bed, tore off her blouse and bra. Her gaze shot to him, impatience etched on her face. "Did you not understand what I said? Strip. Now. I have some serious thanking to do. In a most delicious way."

"Hell yes!"

For the Love of His Cowgirl

The sound of water running and Amber's off-key singing pulled Adam from the bare edges of sleep. He opened one eyelid and glanced at the digital clock next to him. Not quite five o'clock in the morning. What the heck was she doing up already? Wasn't it Saturday? Didn't they sleep in on the weekends? Oh yeah, that had been in his *other* life.

He rolled to his stomach and pulled a pillow over his head. Sleep. He really, really needed it. Instead of sleeping, he'd spent the night mentally going over the specs for the new breeding plan and the new horse barn. It seemed like his brain never had a chance to shut down anymore. There was always one issue or another to take care of on a ranch. It was wearing him down.

Tune it all out. Forget the ranch for another hour or so. Ignore your naked wife in there under the shower, water dripping over that sweet body. Shut down.

Instead he thought about how they'd been excited to move here to his family's ranch this summer. *Been* being the key word for him. Amber still was. His enthusiasm had faded after the first couple of months and a lot of sore muscles. No, he supposed, he was still enthusiastic, he was just tired. It had been a lot easier being the accountant for the family ranch and living in Oklahoma City. He'd been satisfied playing at being a cowboy now and then. But when he and his sister had put their dad in a nursing home, they'd needed to figure out what to do with the ranch. He'd honestly been tempted to sell it, even if this had been the Powell Ranch for almost two hundred years. Amber and Josie had ganged up on him, worn him down. So here he was, back where he'd grown up and sworn he wouldn't ever live again.

He sighed. His brain started getting fuzzy. He'd almost managed to nod off when the bathroom door opened and light hit him where the pillow failed to cover his head. He scowled and started to tug the pillow lower when he caught sight of Amber in the doorway. She was all curvy, naked woman. *His* naked woman.

She looked straight at him, clearly aware that she had his full attention. She stood there so damn tempting, slowly brushing the blonde hair that fell nearly to her waist. His mouth watered. *Want, desire, need* fired through him. And the brat knew it. She went right on brushing her hair, smiling sassily at him.

"Stop teasing me," he growled, turning to his side. He tried to remember the last time they'd played any kind of teasing game. Then he tried to remember the last time they'd even made love. Their busy life with everything that needed to be done around the ranch had taken its toll on their marriage. He was weighted down with responsibilities. "Come here."

She took her sweet time putting the brush down, stopping to turn on the light by the dresser, and then strolling toward him. The sight of her wearing nothing but a crooked smile and a hint of mischief in her eyes was killing him. He had a bad feeling about this. It was clear that she was in the mood to have her way with him, including torturing him. *Sweet brat.*

"So, cowboy, ready for a ride?" She stopped close to his side of the bed, toyed with some long strands of her hair that teased one of her nipples. Smiling, she casually thumbed that nipple and it pebbled.

He swallowed hard, unable to look away from where she flicked the nipple again. He shoved the covers aside and shifted until he sat on the edge of the bed. "I'd been thinking how I needed to get up and going for the day, but it appears my cowgirl has something else in mind." He did, too, although he sure shouldn't.

Her gaze heated and she focused on his thick, morning erection standing tall and get-your-butt-over-here proud. "It's been a while and I've missed my boy toy."

"Your 'boy toy' has missed you, too." He reached down to rub his cock as it swelled even more.

Her pretty pink tongue slipped out to run over the crease of her heart-shaped mouth. She knew he liked it when she did that. Her eyes danced with mischief. Then she moved one of her hands to the apex of her legs. Holding his gaze, she eased her fingers toward the place he ached to be inside.

"Oh, sweetheart, you're really in a mood, aren't you?" He thought he just might explode if he didn't touch her soon. And the imp knew it, amusement tipping up the corners of her mouth. "Come here," he demanded with more urgency.

Of course she didn't obey. His stubborn wife only obeyed when it suited her. She didn't step an inch closer, simply moved enough to shift her legs slightly apart and continued sliding her fingers between her legs. Her nostrils flared from the stimulation and he could smell her arousal.

Her hand stopped and she grinned mischievously as she pushed a finger inside her. A look of pleasure flittered in her expression. "Is that an order?"

He wanted to pull that finger to his mouth, suck the taste of her off it. He wanted to drive his shaft deep where that finger had been. *His place.*

Heaven…Hell. He was caught somewhere in between. She danced her fingertips along her soft folds, sighed quietly, her nostrils flaring even more.

He groaned, gripping his throbbing shaft tighter. One stroke of his hand and a bead of cum dribbled from his cockhead. It had been too damn long since he'd felt her squeezing all around him, enfolding him within that delicious warmth, encouraging him. At this rate, he wasn't going to last much longer.

"Get your ass over here, cowgirl," he growled, pumping his rod once again. "It's time to saddle up."

Ornery woman that she was, she still didn't move closer. She simply began caressing one breast and fingering her cunt with the other hand. He struggled to pull in a breath watching her, pumping his cock again and again.

After a few seconds, she trembled. Her eyes started to glaze over in her obvious excitement. "What if I don't?" she asked in a sensual tease.

He let go of his cock and stretched out to pull her to him. The familiar scent of her, the heat in her gaze, made his heart pound. He reached around her naked body and cupped her ass with his hands. She leaned against him, putting her breasts at mouth level, making them so damn tempting.

Instead of tasting those plump beauties, he squeezed her butt cheeks. "I'm thinking you need a good fucking." Only when they played did he talk coarsely to her. Any other time he was a gentleman cowboy and she was his lady. "A long, hard, make you scream fucking."

She moaned, eyes widening. Her hardened nipples pressed against him. "Are you man enough?" she whispered the challenge.

"You doubt me?" He bit down on the closest nipple enough to make her suck in a breath. Pleased, he rolled his tongue around it, before leaning back to look at her. "Damn right I am."

She shivered within his hold and threaded her fingers into his hair. "Prove it, cowboy."

With a grin, he pinched the taut bud, again enjoying her quiet gasp. As she focused on him, he applied both hands to her soft ass, massaging the quivering cheeks. Again, she sighed, leaned into him He loved how she easily responded to whatever he did. His thoughts shifted in another direction. "I'm thinking this butt needs some attention of a different kind. A nice warming to start off this cold December day."

She nibbled his ear, which always upped his interest, something she well knew. Brat. Then she giggled and looked at him with pure sin dancing in her eyes. "Have I been a naughty cowgirl?" she asked in a sexy, seductive tone. The one that always made him even hotter.

He slapped one buttock hard enough to make her hiss, make her eyes darken. "I'm hoping you'll get a lot naughtier," he said on a husky breath. "Have your wicked way with me."

"You should be careful what you ask for." She pushed him backward, grinning as he blinked up at her. "Move, cowboy. I've got a serious need to..." She winked and he couldn't scramble back fast enough.

Amber felt boneless as she stretched atop her sweaty, exhausted husband. *Wow!* The last half hour or so had definitely been "wow" time. She didn't want to move, wasn't sure she even could. Her big guy was so nice and comfortable beneath her, her personal heated pillow. She'd missed times like this.

She sighed as the pleasure faded and her thoughts turned depressed. They used to play exciting little games, shared fantasies, and acted out scenarios. She'd even worn the occasional sexy costume for him. What had happened to them? When had they become so ho-hum boring?

He reached around her to toy with her hair, something they both enjoyed. It sent a frisson of awareness through her. "I wondered if you were still alive," she teased and raised her head to look at him.

Her long hair brushed against the sides of her breasts, draped over his excellent chest.

"Barely." He blew out a deep breath, making her move up and down with his body. "I'm not as young as I used to be. I may have to take the day off to recover."

She rolled her eyes at his exaggeration. "You're thirty-five, not with one foot in the grave." She couldn't resist squirming a little over him, relishing the feel of every hard-muscled inch of him. Then she giggled as she felt the stirrings of another erection. No, he most definitely wasn't too old for this. "Can't get enough, huh?"

"Boy Wonder may be interested in going another round, but it's not happening." He stroked her hair again and looked grimly at her. "Both of us have chores to get to. Then I've got to run into the feed store and pick up that load of grain we ordered yesterday."

Disappointment wound through her. His "boy wonder" was swelling in spite of what Adam had said. She was a bit sore, but she would certainly go another round...or two. "Are you sure?" She moved ever so slowly against him, trying to change his mind. "Really sure?"

Annoyance etched his beard roughened face. He gave her bare bottom a brisk smack. "Stop that! You can't always get your way."

The swat had stung and she frowned at him. "But we're already conveniently naked. Already here in this nice big, warm bed." She heard the pout in her voice, which she knew he wouldn't like. But, darn it, who knew when they would get around to doing this again! It had been a month or more since the last time they'd come together for more than a quick wham-bam-thank-you-ma'am moment.

"I know you want to." She wriggled over him again, determined to tempt him into staying right where they were.

His big hand settled over the spot he'd just swatted, in warning not in play. "Don't you have a full schedule training those new saddle horses today? It's only a week until Christmas. Aren't those horses supposed to be ready for their owners by then?"

Her body tingled beneath his calloused palm. She'd been serious. She desperately wanted to spend more time heating up the sheets. "Yes. But taking another hour wouldn't be that big a deal." Her whine had grown and she heard the quiet grinding of his teeth.

She should accept the situation, but logic wasn't with her at the moment. There was an unquenchable need inside her this morning.

Irritation laced her words as she asked, "Am I really so resistible to you? Is that why it has been so long since we've had steamy sex?" Sure, he'd gotten all hot and bothered just minutes ago, but *she* had been the one to initiate it.

He smacked her butt harder this time and his expression had turned stony. "Is that what you really think? That I don't *want* you?"

She shrugged. "Well, it seems like it."

"Neither of us has an hour to spare today," he reminded her in his rational tone. "This isn't the time to get into an argument about how much I want to fuck you. And, *yes*, I do want that. But I don't like being manipulated and you know that."

She blew out a breath of frustration. When he set his mind on something, there wasn't much she could do to change it. He lived by a strict schedule, making only small allowances to spur of the moment things that came up. She was actually surprised he'd stayed in bed so long this morning. And she was very glad for the way she'd had his undivided attention for at least a little while. Yet she didn't want to give up just yet.

"Maybe it's time," she boldly dared.

His hand had settled on her butt again, holding her in place. He gave a squeeze of caution. Ridiculous as it was, her stomach fluttered. Her clit pulsed with interest. Her body wanted anything he would give her. She remembered how he'd mentioned giving her a nice bottom warming to start off this cold winter day. That didn't sound so terrible. Particularly if it led to…well, getting her way.

"Up, sweetheart," he ordered in a sharp tone, arching upward to get her to move.

What was that old saying? *In for a penny, in for a pound.* Well, she'd gotten her penny's worth of delectable attention from him. Now she wanted the rest of the pound's worth. As with sex between them lately, spankings had been rare, too. He believed in discipline for certain infractions to agreed-upon rules or acts of misbehavior. She wasn't wild about them, but accepted them, although not always gracefully. Was he so darn busy with the ranch that he couldn't take some of his precious time to deal with disciplining her? Why hadn't she thought about this before? Okay, not going to bed with a sore butt was a good thing. Still…

"About that bottom warming you mentioned." She ignored the way her face heated and she looked directly at him, jutted out her chin in challenge.

His brow furrowed and stress lines creased the corners of his mouth. "I wasn't serious."

Her heart pounded. This was nuts. *Forget this crazy idea!* Instead she blew out a frustrated breath. "Maybe I want it."

His eyes narrowed in disapproval. "You *want* me to spank you?"

No! "Yes." There! She'd said it, okay practically begged for it.

"We don't have time for this nonsense, Amber Powell. I've got things to do. You've got things to do. We didn't really even have time for—"

"So you just humored me!" she cut him off. "You didn't think we even had time for that quick hump and bump. You just fucked me so I wouldn't nag you?" Now she was hurt and mad.

She shoved her way off his chest and climbed off the bed. "I'm sorry to have bothered you. It won't happen again," she said primly.

Before she could take more than a step away, he snapped, "Watch your language, young lady! And you're being ridiculous."

Squaring her shoulders, she hissed, "You said *fuck* first."

He gave a curt nod. "Still, I don't like such crassness crossing your lips." His expression tight, he added, "Since you really want a spanking, I'll give you one."

"Don't do me any favors." She stood still, trembling in anger and irritation, her eyes stinging, and she blinked rapidly. What had gone wrong here? This wasn't what she wanted, not really. But she'd had a moment of insanity and pushed his patience.

"You're acting like a real brat now. For no reason." His shoulders were rigid as he sat again on the side of the bed.

"No reason! I have to beg for a few minutes of your time." She ignored the moisture on her cheeks and swallowed a lump in her throat. He'd hurt her pride and bruised her heart. "As I said, I won't bother you again."

He must have seen the tears, heard the misery in her voice. He cursed. "Dammit, sweetheart, do you really want to start the day off this way?"

She brushed off her cheeks with the back of her hands. "By getting some more of your precious time? I had thought so."

"By getting your ass burned," he countered. He drew in a deep breath and blew it out.

Everything had gone way off course from where she'd intended this to go. She'd been excited when he'd mentioned a bottom warming. But he hadn't been serious, at least not seeing it as a foreplay kind of thing. And in her disappointment she'd turned whiny. He never liked that and neither did she. Talking about burning her ass because she'd annoyed him wasn't good, not at all.

"You're right, we've both got more important things to get to." Was that still a whine in her tone? Maybe he hadn't noticed.

"Get your paddle." He had caught it and she'd pushed the matter too far. When she warily looked at him, his jaw had tightened. He waited.

"How about we start over? We each get up, get ready, and go our separate ways like always." She inwardly groaned at having added the 'like always' comment. Her bitterness about their lifestyle at the moment was evident.

He raised an eyebrow. "Meaning I've been a bad husband lately? That us not burning up the sheets has all been my fault?"

She worried her lower lip. He'd called her bluff and he was right: she'd been as much at fault about their lack of lovemaking recently as him. She shook her head, dread tumbling in her stomach.

"Paddle," he reminded her, not backing down an inch.

"I've got to saddle train today," she protested quietly.

"It's going to be a bit uncomfortable for you." His gaze shifted to the closet where the long, thin paddle hung on a hook. *Her paddle.*

The morning had definitely taken a turn for the worse. Sitting in those saddles today was going to be a lot more than "uncomfortable." But she'd nudged them to this point with her over-worrying about things. She should have just enjoyed what they'd done and treasured those memories the rest of the day. She shouldn't have gotten frustrated with her stressed and tired husband.

She walked in resignation to the closet and took the disliked paddle from the hook. He'd gotten it for her not long after they'd married almost seven years ago. The words *Bad Girl* were fading from use even though he hadn't used it in a while.

When she stepped out of the closet, Adam stood by the dresser. She preferred going over his knee for her punishments. They just seemed better somehow, more personal. Standing with her arms braced on whatever surface while he disciplined her felt more impersonal. But she wasn't the one who picked the when, the how, the where or the how long.

He stood calmly, grimly, as she walked over and handed him the paddle. Without him saying a word, she gripped the edge of the dresser and stepped far enough away that she could lower her head to the top. As she dropped her head, she glanced at their wedding picture. She still loved this man as much as she had when they had said their vows. Even when he burned her bottom.

"What do you think you deserve for the brattiness?" He shifted to her left side.

She knew he already had a number of swats in mind, but she answered him anyway. "Five." That seemed reasonable, bearable for being on a saddle later.

"I'm thinking a dozen sounds better."

A dozen. Not good. She tensed for the first swat, never his hardest.

When it came, she released the breath she'd held. Not so bad. She eased her grip on the dresser for a second and then held her breath for the next one. *This* would be the attention getter.

She heard the whisper of sound as the paddle came at her. It landed briskly and she gasped, arching her back. Yes, he had her attention. Geez, it stung so much already!

"Ten more. Hold real still, sweetheart. I'll get these done right quick and we'll be good to go."

"Good to go? Hold still? Damn easy for you to say." She gritted her teeth, tensing again. He'd have taken care of this "unpleasant chore"—as he called it—and would go on about his day.

He blazed the paddle down briskly five times before he gave her a breather. She danced from foot to foot, gripping the dresser's edge tight, quietly hissing after each strike.

"Almost done."

The sting settled in and she wanted the rest of the swats already delivered. Again, she thought about how after this that the problem for him would be taken care of. He'd give her a brief comforting hug and go shower, get dressed, and tend to his business. She would have to deal with a burning butt, the awfulness of pulling on jeans, and then walking around all day as the tight denim rubbed against her sore bottom. It took longer for the pain to go away when she couldn't just lie on the bed and let it fade. Bouncing in a saddle would bring all these "wonderful" feelings back over and over.

Another sharp swat jarred her out of her musings. She gritted out, "Damn!" Then she quickly said, "Sorry. I wasn't focused."

She took the final four swats with as much grace as she could. Only with the last sizzling one did she arch backward and cry out, "Owwww!" She sucked in a shuddery breath. Gawd, it hurt.

Next came the awkward moment of standing upright, wincing at the discomfort of moving. She drew in several deep, steadying breaths before she turned to face him. As usual, he gave her a gentle look. He'd once told her that he didn't like causing her even minor pain, but sometimes it was necessary.

"I'll take a quick shower." He pulled her into the expected hug and walked quietly to the bathroom. He stopped and glanced back at her. "Are we still on for going to Tom and Sally's party tonight?"

Perfect. A paddling, a day's worth of discomfort, and they had a Christmas get-together to attend tonight. She wasn't really in a festive spirit. But she nodded before she went to hang up her paddle.

****

Mid-afternoon Adam drove back into the ranch yard from town. The day had been killer long and they still had a party to attend tonight. He yawned.

He'd sure rather stay home and snuggle with Amber. What she'd started this morning had played over and over in his head all day long. The way she'd taken his cock into her hot mouth, drove him to the brink of pouring down her throat. But she'd stopped at the opportune time and straddled him. It hadn't taken her but a couple of slow sensuous glides down his cock before he'd given her his all. Not that things had ended there. Oh, no, his determined wife had kept at him.

Of course, he'd more than cooperated. It might not have taken all that long, but he'd given her a damn good fucking, like he'd promised her.

He hadn't realized how much he'd missed messing around with her. He missed more than just the sex. He'd almost forgotten how playful she could be and how much he liked the spirited side of her. They'd both been too damn busy, going their separate ways too much. They came to bed late at night and crashed. He couldn't remember the last time they'd even cuddled before they fell asleep.

Disgusted with himself, he yanked the key out of the ignition and ground his jaw. His marriage was fading away and he hadn't even noticed. He'd been taking Amber for granted. *Damn.*

A man shouldn't assume his wife was happy just because she didn't complain all the time. She *had* complained this morning and he'd spanked her for it. He'd been too stressed, too…well, too everything. She'd deserved a few swats with his hand, but not getting her butt paddled.

The ranch demanded too much of his focus. He needed to shift more of the responsibilities to his foreman. Jake was a good ranch hand and he'd worked here more years than he had. He needed to spend more time with the woman he loved.

Jake walked over to the truck and Adam climbed out. "I'll let you men deal with these supplies."

He nodded toward the truck's bed filled with bags of feed, some fencing, and other boxes of supplies they'd ordered. He shut the cab door. "You and I need to have a talk after Christmas. I want to discuss some changes in duties, you taking on more."

"Sure, boss." Jake grinned. "I'm up for it." He waved at a couple of ranch hands coming out of the barn. "You and Amber still going to Tom's later? She's looking a bit tired today."

Guilt curled through him. No doubt she was tired from all the early physical activity, including the paddling he'd given her. She'd gotten snippy, tried to manipulate him, which she knew he didn't like. But he didn't have to wallop her like that. He'd known she would have a tough day ahead with helping to saddle break the horses. It had to have been damn uncomfortable for her today.

He pulled himself back to the moment. "I'm not sure if we'll go or not."

Jake walked behind the truck. "I think she's still in the indoor arena."

Adam wasn't sure he wanted to face her right now, but told himself to man-up and do it. He didn't want to see her flinching in discomfort as she worked the horses. But then maybe she wasn't flinching anymore, maybe the sting had faded away. After all, he hadn't given her that much of a paddling.

As he walked into the large arena where they trained horses during the winter, he was relieved to find his wife standing along the metal railing and not sitting a horse. Her attention was focused on a couple of the younger ranch hands working with two of the mares. But she looked stiff and he noticed a wince when she shifted from foot to foot. Her hands moved subtly back to rub her bottom. Not a good sign.

"Are you almost done for the day?" he asked, moving closer,

cautiously.

She glanced at him in surprise. Her face turned pink and she dropped her hands from her butt. "I'm done riding, yes." She turned toward the arena and lowered her voice. "It was worse than I thought it would be. All that lifting up and settling back down…kind of like getting paddled all over again."

He wasn't on her "good" list at the moment. "How about I call Tom and tell them we aren't coming tonight? We can just stay home, maybe watch a movie." *Let me make it up to you.*

"If I can suffer with a sore bottom all day doing this, I can certainly go to a party. They're our closest friends. We need to go." She didn't look at him. "Don't you have some bookwork to do? Some calls to make?"

He didn't like her trying to get rid of him, even if he did need to get on the ranch computer for a while. "I'm sorry, sweetheart. You pressed my last nerve and paid the price. I shouldn't have paddled your ass." But she needed a reminder that she'd pushed him at a bad time. "A spanking would have been enough."

She glanced at him, puzzled. "I didn't ask for an apology." She turned away again. "I've moved on from that."

* * * *

Christmas Eve. Amber couldn't believe how fast the last week had gone. The horses she'd been hired to saddle break were trained and gone. She'd earned more than she'd figured on and she'd spent every last penny. On things for Adam. He could be something of a penny pincher at times, but it came naturally for an accountant, she supposed. But he didn't care how she spent *her* money, money that she earned separate from the normal ranch income.

He wasn't home yet and she was worried about him. He'd gotten a cold the day after they'd had that ridiculous argument. Not wanting to expose her more than necessary, he'd slept in the spare bedroom. She'd protested, but he'd insisted. Big, stubborn cowboy.

Cold or not, he'd worked alongside the hands as they'd mended some fences. And he'd helped several of the local ranchers with some end-of-the year accounting in his limited spare time. Again, she'd tried to convince him to wait on the bookkeeping stuff until after the first of the year. But, no, he'd gone all pig-headed about that, too.

Where is he? She looked anxiously out the bedroom window. A thin layer of snow covered the ground and big, fat flakes were falling. Not a snowstorm to worry about, just enough to make it pretty for Christmas. But the wind was blowing and seeped in around the blinds making her shiver. If she had on more clothes, it probably wouldn't bother her.

Headlights turning off the ranch road and into the yard caught her attention. Her heart skipped a beat and excitement thrummed through her. He was finally home. She had a hot meal of his favorite chili in the Crockpot, corn bread, too. She'd bought his beer of choice as well. And she'd even made pecan pie from his mother's recipe. She wanted everything to be perfect tonight. She knew he still loved her, the fire of it had dwindled some and tonight she intended to get it going all over again.

She felt as nervous as when she'd first met him. She'd wanted to impress the brother of her college roommate, having decided he was the man she wanted from the instant she'd seen his picture. That ruggedly carved, handsome face with his sky blue eyes and jet-black hair had called to her. *Mine, mine, mine.* She'd thought that then, and she felt that way now.

Slowly she made her way down the stairs. The tree lights were on and the tree and all of the decorations she'd put up looked beautiful. It had taken her all day to put everything out and decorate the tree. His family had always waited to put up their tree on Christmas Eve, a tradition which she was ready to change. She wanted to enjoy it for more than a few days. Hopefully he would be okay with her idea.

She heard the garage door opening and closing and hurried into the great room. She settled onto one of the large floor pillows she'd moved next to the tree. Then she waited.

Adam strode into the kitchen and inhaled the scent of spicy chili. He was glad he could smell again. Damn cold had felt like it had lasted forever.

A glance toward the small table by the window had him spotting two place settings and a pecan pie. His stomach growled. Amber had gone to a lot of trouble for him and he knew he didn't deserve it. After he'd sworn to himself that he would spend more time with her, life had gotten even crazier. And he'd gotten a cold. He'd spent most of this last week sleeping in the second bedroom, and he'd hated it. But he'd been determined not to give her his cold if he could help it. Tonight he'd move back to their bedroom. Assuming she'd let him.

He lifted the lid off the crockpot and drew in the scent of beef, peppers, and his wife's other secret ingredients. A pan of corn bread sat nearby. She spoiled him, even when they were at odds.

Again his stomach rumbled. But he needed to find her first. He was going to kiss the hell out of her now that he wasn't contagious anymore. Then he was going to...

"I'm in here," he heard her call from the next room.

His heart raced at her familiar voice, at a curious softness in her tone. God, he loved her.

He started forward and then froze. What the hell had he been thinking today? Going into town to meet with a few of the ranchers about some area news. He'd forgotten all about what day it was, all about putting up the Christmas tree. *Damn, damn, damn.* He'd let his wife down.

He patted his pocket and the envelope he had there. Hopefully what he'd bought her would go a ways toward showing her how much she meant to him.

Braced for seeing her and disappointment on her beautiful face, he stepped into the great room. Christmas had taken over. His mother's nativity set and collection of angels sat on the mantel. He'd almost forgotten about them since his father hadn't put them out in the few years since she'd died. Stockings were hung and looked stuffed, but he couldn't imagine with what. Most amazingly, she had put up their tree and decorated it. She'd gone to all of this effort for him...for them. His heart swelled with so much love for her that he feared it would burst.

Then he spotted her sitting just to the side of the tree. How had he not noticed her first? He really was out of it. But, admittedly, the rest had taken him by surprise. She sat on a big pillow, wearing a barely-there, white fringy outfit of some kind. Her breasts nearly toppled out of the skimpy bodice and the sides were cut deeply, showing a lot of bare skin. She wore a white wide-brimmed hat and short white boots. *His cowgirl.*

"I hope..." He had to clear his throat and start again. "I hope you aren't planning on wearing that get-up for long." He was going to rip it off of her in about another minute.

His sexy wife put her hands down and casually lifted the front of the skirt, which was really all just fringe. No panties. Not even a thong. "We don't even have to wait for you to take this off me."

His palms were sweating. His cock was demanding freedom, ready to drive deep between those amazing legs. There was so much he wanted to say to her. He'd practiced it on the way home, couldn't seem to remember a damn word of it now.

He walked straight to her and went down on his knees. "Don't ever leave me." He'd been worrying about that for days.

She blinked. "Why would I do that? You're the other half of me." She gave him a sassy grin. "Maybe *not* the best half. But I wouldn't be whole without you."

He closed his eyes for a second, then looked at her, and his heart swelled. "I'm going to change things around here. Jake will take on more responsibilities. I'll have more time, I promise. Time I plan to spend with you."

Her lower lip wobbled and she bit down on it. He reached out to touch her mouth and heard the crinkle of the paper in his coat pocket. He hadn't even taken off his jacket yet in his need to find her. Uncertainly he pulled the envelope out and handed it to her.

"It's tickets for a Caribbean cruise, next spring." He couldn't wait for her to open it, had to tell her. "We were going to do it for our honeymoon, but I chickened out. Worried about getting seasick. But there's a patch for that, I hear."

She smiled, tears sparkling in her eyes. She put a finger to his mouth to stop him from rambling. "I love you so much. Even more because you're willing to do that for me." Then she laughed softly and reached behind her to something she'd obviously stuck in the tree. "Like minds...sort of."

Confused, he accepted the envelope she pushed at him. Just as he'd done, she didn't wait for him to open it. "Tickets to the Super Bowl."

He gaped at her. "No kidding? The Super Bowl?" He pulled her into his arms and hugged her so tightly she squeaked. Easing up, he said, "You're the best wife ever, and I'm never letting you go."

She flipped off her hat. "Are you going to take off your coat and stay awhile? Maybe take off everything else, too?" She waggled an eyebrow at him. "You want to cowboy-up this time? Or am I going all cowgirl-gone-wild again?"

He began yanking off his clothes, breathing hard, so damn ready for anything and everything. "Not that I don't enjoy you going *cowgirl wild*, but I'm taking charge this time."

She peeled off her outfit, grinning. "I was hoping you'd say that."

Cowboys and Their Toys

Jennifer's head pounded as she watched Jason walk out of the bathroom, a towel slung low across his hips. He'd already showered and shaved. All she'd done was lay here in bed, her body slowly recovering. Her cowboy had woken up early this morning, not to get started with ranch chores. No, he'd had a serious hard-on and a major desire to play games. She didn't mind his wilder times really, but sometimes he pushed the edge. This had been one of those days, particularly since she had a hangover.

He gave her a cocky grin, his brown-eyed gaze intense as he regarded her. She was still where he'd left her, tied spread-eagled across their bed. "You look so damn irresistible this way, sweetheart." He ambled closer, reaching down to trail his fingertips up one inner thigh and down the other. As she trembled, he blew out a ragged breath as well. "Mine, all mine."

He'd spent over an hour proving just how much he was in control when he tied her down. The things he could do with those big, long-fingered hands. The ways he could torture her with his talented tongue. She'd nearly passed out from blind pleasure at one point. Then he'd fucked her so hard she'd thought the bed would collapse. After he'd calmed enough to be able to move again, he'd climbed off of her, gotten a wet rag and cleaned her up, but he hadn't released her before taking his shower. She knew he liked seeing her at his mercy as long as possible. For the most part, she was okay with it. She'd accepted his dominant ways even before they married four years ago.

His gaze continued to hold her, possessively. As ridiculous as it was, she blushed all over.

This had never been a lifestyle she'd dreamed about. If any other man had suggested trying the simplest part of BDSM, she would have turned him down before he could take another breath. With Jason, though… She'd trusted him to be careful with her. She'd come a long way since the first time he'd tied her hands together.

"I didn't hurt you, did I?" Concern creased his brow. His quickly towel-dried hair looked sleep rumpled. She liked threading her fingers through the thick, dark hair and wanted to touch it even now.

"Did I?" he asked again, frowning at her lack of response.

"No." She'd thought she might die, being taken from one shattering orgasm to another. But *hurt* her? No, he hadn't.

A masculine smugness replaced the concern. He stroked her inner thighs again; whisper soft, smiling wickedly as she quivered from head to toe. "So responsive," he said in approval.

She liked that she pleased him. Sometimes, though, she wondered if she could actually do what he wanted to try. So far she'd never let him down and enjoyed the times when he pushed her limits. But he'd been hinting about taking things a bit deeper, to a more extreme level. She'd balked at the suggestion so far. He hadn't pressed her about it in the last couple of weeks, but she was pretty sure the idea was still in his head. The worrier in her feared that if she didn't agree to it, he'd lose interest in her.

There were a lot of women around who would very much want her hard-bodied, sexy husband. She still had trouble believing he'd gone after her, a somewhat shy part-time teacher instead of one of the more aggressive women in town.

Forcing her thoughts back to the moment, she said casually, "It's time, don't you think? You're going to be late meeting your friends in town." She had a lot to do too. "And I need to get started on my Christmas baking."

Normally she would have just asked him to let her up now. But she'd gotten in trouble with him last night at the local ranchers' party. She'd had too much to drink and gotten to be a lot more "party girl" than he liked. Then during the drive home, she'd been foolish enough to sass him about his being a stick in the mud. He'd ended up burning the blazes out of her butt with the "learning" paddle before they went to bed. Her having a tender bottom this morning hadn't kept him from this wild session. Of course, she'd enjoyed herself. But her bottom was sore again from all the frantic bouncing around and rubbing against the sheets.

He considered her eyes, frowning. "Still a bit hungover, aren't you?" He moved down to untie one foot and then the other. "I hope you got the message last night about not drinking yourself silly. We've got more parties this week. I don't want to have to deliver another walloping or two."

She didn't want that either. "No more liquor for me," she vowed. She drew her legs closer together and sighed in relief.

"I don't mind if you drink, Jen. You just need to pay more attention to the number of drinks you down." He untied her wrists, taking a second to gently massage each one before gently kissing it.

Her arms tingled, but not from having been restrained so long. There always seemed to be magic in his touches, his kisses. She couldn't get enough of them.

But there would be no more now. He nodded at the bathroom, his expression grim. "Go tend to your personal business. I'll get dressed and then we'll deal with the other matter."

"Other matter?" Her heart raced. He must have told her about another punishment after he'd finished paddling her and she'd laid down crying herself to sleep. He'd been really upset with her. And she did remember calling him a name or two. She only did that when she got drunk and careless with her tongue.

He opened the top drawer of the nightstand next to the bed. She didn't want to see what he was going to pull out. Yet she couldn't look away. Dread curled through her at the sight of the anal plug he used when she'd really misbehaved.

"You know I didn't mean what I said," she said warily. "We don't have to…" But she knew him. He had made up his mind to do this and it was going to happen.

His answer was to toss the plug on the bed and walk to the closet for his clothes.

She thought about staying in the bathroom but she knew that delaying the matter would only upset him more. She'd earned this punishment and she would live with it.

He was fully dressed by the time she walked out again. He held a tube of lube in one hand and the intimidating plug in the other. "Bend over. Let's get this done with since we both have things to get to today."

Her day would be much better without walking around with a plug up her ass. She could refuse it. Jason never insisted on something she didn't agree to do. But she was a submissive and accepted that fact. She loved him, even the stern dominant side of him. Resigned, she stood next to the bed and bent over to brace her hands on the mattress. She felt so vulnerable in this position, with her bottom thrust high for him, with him seeing her most private areas.

"Ease your feet apart a little more." As she did so, he carefully applied the lubrication around her hole and just inside it. She clenched uncomfortably at the coldness. While she adjusted and waited, he took another second to apply lube to the plug as well. Then he separated her cheeks with one hand, held them apart, and guided the tip of the plug to her rim. "Hold still, sweetheart."

Her stomach tightened at the warning. No matter how many ways he'd seen her naked and spread, having him shove a large rubber plug in her ass was embarrassing. She held her breath at first. He worked it in an inch, pulled it almost out, pushed it in further. He always gave her time to adjust. The point of making her wear a punishment plug wasn't to hurt her, but to give her a reason *not* to act in a specific way again. It was a difficult lesson to endure.

"Ready?" He held the plug still just barely inside her rectum and waited for her answer.

She could still say *no* and he would stop. She'd never done that to test him, but she knew he would. Dragging this out any longer only made it worse. "Yes."

He pressed harder and the plug went past her sensitized sphincter muscles. She grimaced in discomfort as her body took over and pulled the horrible object the rest of the way inside. *So full. So awful.* The initial sting always made her suck in a breath, just as it did now.

"Okay?" he asked cautiously. Even if she deserved to be punished, he always let her know he cared about her.

"Yes," she hissed. The first sting started fading, but the fullness and oddness would remain for as long as she was required to wear the plug. Sometimes he only made her keep it in for an hour or so. Sometimes it was all day. Once it had been for all night.

She didn't move, still adapting to the alien object inside her ass. "How long?" she gritted out.

He'd walked away and returned to carefully lift one foot and then the other into a pair of tight-fitting exercise shorts. He'd bought them for her specifically for keeping a plug in her bottom as she moved around. He eased them up her legs, drawing her upright, and then patting between her legs to make sure the plug was still in place. "We'll take it out tonight."

Oh, god, all day! She grew edgy, her stomach knotted with dread. The tiny movement made the plug immediately press harder inside her. She wanted to protest, tell him again how sorry she was for her bad behavior. But she didn't want to disappoint him more. Part of why she didn't want to wear the plug was it had a tendency to make her sensitive, to arouse her. Already she was feeling the stirring of desire. It would be worse when she actually moved.

She tried not to think about it, but it was impossible to forget the discomfort she experienced. "We have a dinner at the church tonight."

He met her gaze, a firm disciplinarian now. "Make sure it's still in when I come home. If it is…" He didn't have to say that if it wasn't, he'd put it back and she'd be wearing it to church. It had happened before. That wasn't something she wanted to have happen again.

"I'll be good." But it would be difficult.

* * * *

Jason sat across from two of his neighboring ranchers in Bev's Coffee and Donut shop like he did almost every Monday morning. It was their "catch up" time. They talked about what was going on in the county and they discussed the state of the poor cattle market. Usually he was a big part of the conversation. Today he couldn't keep focused on what they said. His thoughts were twenty miles away on the woman he loved so much he hurt sometimes from the strength of his feelings. How had he ever gotten so damn lucky to find Jennifer?

"Have you even heard a word I said?" Walker asked, sounding annoyed.

"I'm thinking he's a mighty satisfied man this morning." Pete winked at him. "I'm envious as hell. What with my wife being about ready to explode with child any minute."

Walker shook his head, frowning. "Have pity on me, you two. I'm still reeling from the divorce from Hell. I don't even want to think about sex with another woman."

"Well, only Jason here is getting any these days anyway." Pete scooped up some scrambled eggs with a slice of toast. "I guess you got over being mad at Jennifer about last night."

Jason nodded, although he was still irritated. "We've moved on."

He wasn't happy about giving her a sound walloping last night, but she'd gotten out of control. Going to bed with a hot butt and sobbing a little always calmed her down. It meant they didn't make love, either. But he'd done that before dawn this morning. Okay, he'd gone to bed horny and his dreams had been double X-rated. So he'd needed something extra fiery and tying her up always made him a wild man. She'd barely hinted at protesting. She was learning. He thought he'd made it clear that he wouldn't put up with her going against him.

"Are you going to the church dinner tonight?" Pete asked with a wiggle of his eyebrows. "Or are you two spending some quality time together?"

"Jeez, Pete, you need to get laid," Walker complained.

Jason hadn't had to be celibate any length of time yet, thank God. He knew his friend had been suffering during these last couple of difficult months of his wife's pregnancy. He didn't look forward to suffering that way, but he did want to start a family with Jen. They'd wanted to settle into the marriage a few years. She'd wanted to substitute teach a while longer. But maybe it was time they started getting serious about making babies.

"Reckon you're right," Pete interrupted his thoughts. "The moment the doctor gives her the okay after she's delivered, I'm going to finally get *real* relief."

Jason stayed out of the conversation and took a bite of ham. Having a baby would be a big change in their lives. He liked being more or less her sole focus. He liked having her all to himself. He'd have to learn to share with a child in the picture. But he'd adjust.

He thought again about how deliciously tempting she'd looked all spread-eagled on their bed. His cock hardened in an instant. Under the table, he subtly shifted his package. They would probably have to give up that sort of thing with kids around. He'd have to stop a lot of the little games he liked. But would she mind giving them up? He'd begun to worry lately that she was unhappy with his games. She sure hadn't reacted as well as he'd hoped when he'd mentioned trying the Master/slave thing. He'd really like to take this 24/7, with certain concessions for when she was out in public. But she'd cringed at the idea of even wearing a collar around the house, a collar-like necklace anywhere else. He wasn't giving up, though.

Speaking about "fun," she would be getting extremely aroused by now. He knew what moving around with a plug up her ass did to her. He hadn't really meant to make her wear it all day, certainly not tonight. He just wanted her good and excited when he strolled into the house later this morning. He wanted her to attack him, go all crazy woman on him. She'd done it before a few times and Lord a'mighty they were unforgettable experiences. But she mostly tended to be reserved, uneasy when that side of her came out. He wanted to break her of her worries.

His pulse raced and he needed to shift again. *Think about something else.*

"So, Pete, what did you get Annie for Christmas?" He still hadn't gone shopping for Jen. Time was running out with Christmas Eve only five days away. He didn't have a clue what to get her.

Pete grinned at him. "Meaning you're hunting for ideas for Jennifer. You haven't gotten her anything yet, have you?"

"Shopping for a woman's hard. If I get her clothes in the wrong size or wrong color, then I don't know enough about her. If I buy her some small appliance, that's too impersonal." He hated the whole shopping thing, for Christmas, her birthday, or their anniversary.

"Don't *I* know that!" Pete commiserated. "I got Annie a pretty purple robe last year. She hates purple, I learned. She asked me if I had ever seen her in purple. Damned if I could remember. But it looked pretty."

He took a bite of toast. "Her mom took pity on me this year and told me Annie collects teapots. Hell if I remembered seeing them around the house until she said that. So I bought her two."

Jason studied his coffee. *Did Jen collect anything that he hadn't paid attention to?* She did like to wear jewelry. That much he knew. He'd stop in at one of the jewelry stores in Topeka in a day or so. He needed to go pick up a couple of gifts for his men, too. Maybe new hats or gloves. Something practical.

He realized his cock had finally settled down so he could get up without embarrassing himself. He pulled out his wallet and some money to toss on the table. "My share. I need to go. Chores to get to and I want to see how those cookies Jen's making are going."

Pete snorted. "Sure, whatever you say. We all know what you're really going home for."

Walker just sighed and focused on his breakfast.

* * * *

Where the hell was he? Jennifer pulled another batch of snickerdoodles from the oven. She'd already made two dozen cherry-chocolate cookies, three dozen oatmeal-raisin cookies, and now three dozen snickerdoodles. And she was so crazy turned-on that she could barely think straight. She just hoped she'd put in the right ingredients, in the right quantities.

She set the cookie sheet down and closed her eyes, trying to will the tingling between her legs to stop. The press of that plug didn't give her any relief. The instant he walked in the door she was making him remove it. Then she was taking him to the floor right here in the kitchen.

She'd no sooner made the vow than she heard the garage door opening and the deep rumbling sound of his truck's hemi engine. Her heart did all kinds of little 'yippie!' skips. Her clit throbbed and she could hardly stand still to wait for him to come find her.

As nonchalant as she could be, she turned the oven off and picked up the cookie sheet to slide the new batch of cookies onto the cooling racks. *Hurry! Hurry! Hurry!* If he didn't get in here soon, she was going out to drag him inside.

"Have you been a good girl?" Jason asked in his deep, rumbling voice from behind her.

Stay cool. Don't... The hell with it! She spun to face him. He'd taken his own sweet time coming to her. He'd removed his coat at the back door, his boots, too. Irritation curled through her. Couldn't he see the frantic need in her eyes? "I need you to take it out. Now."

He didn't usually like being ordered around, except when he knew she was desperate for him. Evidently he sensed that now. He smiled in that suggestive way he had and walked casually toward her. His eyes had darkened, too. His nostrils flared.

He took the time to cup her face and give her a kiss that had her trembling against him. Only when he was good and ready did he step back. "Turn around, sweetheart."

She obeyed instantly, relieved. As she braced her hands on the counter and thrust out her bottom, she saw him reach for an oatmeal cookie. "Hey," she protested.

"I'm getting to it," he mumbled between slow bites. Again, when he was ready, he tugged her shorts down, smoothed his hand over her buttocks, and a second later eased the plug from her tender hole.

She sighed in relief, felt warm stickiness coating her lower lips and her throbbing clit. He took his time fingering away some of the moisture, showing it to her as she faced him.

"Someone is ready for her man." He tossed the plug in the sink and began unbuckling his belt, unbuttoning his jeans with incredible slowness.

"You're taking too long." She'd already yanked off her shorts, drew the T-shirt she'd put on over her head, and threw it aside as well. Her pulse raced. She could barely stand still.

"I love it when you get all impatient." He pulled out his long, thickened cock and stroked it. "But I'm not letting you have your way with me here on the cold kitchen tile."

She stared at the engorged shaft with the blue vein that vined around it. She was desperate to touch the soft skin covering the hardness, more frantic to have it impaling her. What had he said? Not on the kitchen floor.

Frustrated and forcing her thoughts to the problem, she took hold of his free arm and tugged him into the family room. The room was all decorated for Christmas, the tree lights already on. She didn't care about any of that at the moment. She led him right in front of the fireplace with the fire she'd already started. With a glance around, she spotted a small quilt on the back of the sofa. She jerked it to her and tossed it on top of the carpet.

"Happy?" she asked, eager to shove him down and climb on board her husband.

But the stubborn cowboy shook his head. "Slow down, sweetheart. I'm seriously overdressed. Give me a second to shed my clothes."

"I don't care if you're overdressed. Just shove your pants out of the way." She focused on his rod, so thick, so proudly standing out. "I only care about *that*."

"I said to calm yourself." His tone was firm, his expression determined. "I plan to enjoy you skin-to-skin. I'm not going to do a half-ass job of fucking you."

She shivered at the coarseness of his statement. *Fucking* her. The image was more vivid than if he'd simply said *making love*. This would be rough, hard, with all the relentless slamming into her as he took them both to that mindless place of pure bliss.

"Please hurry," she begged, fidgeting. Her whole body thrummed with longing.

The exasperating man grinned and finally tossed his shirt, the last of his clothing, on the sofa. His large calloused hand stroked his shaft again and her mouth watered with the desire to touch him. Her hands shook from the strain of resisting until he would allow it, as he'd trained her.

He bent over to stretch out the quilt. He had a picture-perfect ass, a perfect body from all the physical labor he did as a rancher. She could never get enough of looking at him. Well, unless she was desperate for sex, which she was now. He always seemed to know her feelings, her desire, and he enjoyed testing her, making him move at a snail's pace. She thought she just might die from her heart racing so fast before he did what she was waiting for.

Finally he lay down on his back in the middle of the quilt. He looked up at her in expectance. "Well?"

At last! She wasted no time in going down on her knees to straddle his muscled legs. His cockhead thrust up at her pulsing nether lips. His dark eyes watched her; he kept his arms out at his sides. Sometimes when she did this, he would reach for her breasts, caress them, and knead them until they ached. Sometimes he just lay there, waited to see what she would do, which was what he did this time. It gave her such a thrill when he let her be in complete charge.

Vibrating with need, she found the strength to take her time. She took him in hand, slowly fed his thickness into her more than ready body. She fought back the desperation to sit fully down on him and drive his cock as deep as it could go. As much as she ached to do so, she wanted to savor every second of being in control of him.

Inch by inch she took him inside her. Her heart pounded at the pressing need to move faster, that she resisted. Beneath her, she watched his face contort with his own battle against hurrying things along. He had such incredible strength of will. He was giving her this time and she loved him even more for it. Most of the time he was so dominating, determined to be in charge. This was a gift that she treasured.

But she was ready for the next step. Breathing in quick pants, she slid the rest of the way down his swollen cock until he was completely inside her and his balls were against her ass. She sat up straight, feeling so incredibly full, and looked down at him. His beard-stubbled jaw was clenched and his expression tense. Still, he let her set the pace. What touched her the most was the clear love in his eyes.

Her inner muscles tight around him, she proclaimed, "I love you."

"I know you do." He reached up to cup her hips. "I love you, too, sweetheart." He bucked up, hitting the spot inside her that made her crazy. As she sucked in a breath, quivering, he added, "You give me so much; let me do so much, even when I know you aren't certain about what I demand of you."

His praise meant a lot to her, because sometimes she doubted herself in their special relationship. She smiled at him and slowly lifted up his length, easing almost all the way off, sitting still for a couple of torturous seconds. Again, his face mirrored his determination to not take over, to endure.

When she couldn't stand it any longer, she fully impaled herself once more. He groaned as her muscles tightened around him, squeezed. She watched him through half-closed eyes, every nerve so aware of him, craving him. His own eyes narrowed to slits and his brow furrowed as if in mounting pain.

His jaw clenched and he tightened his grip on her hips. "I don't know how much more I can take," he gritted out. He released her hips, covered her breasts with his strong hands, and made the nipples harden against his palms.

As she leaned forward, her long hair draped over his arms. She loved when he touched her breasts, when he suckled them. But this time he released them all too soon. Disappointment curled through her.

Then he took hold of her hair and tugged her down over him. "That's better."

While she missed his hands on her sensitized breasts, she trembled at the way his cock shifted within her. He was taking charge now and she was ready for that. Proving it, he began pushing upward, forcing her to move.

She moaned. *Heaven. Oh, yes!* At the silent insistence in his gaze, she worked her body up and down his rod, squeezing him tighter each time she slid upward.

When he'd clearly decided to take charge even more, he shifted her beneath him. "My turn."

"Yes, your turn," she purred, desperate for his control.

For just a second he flashed her a smug, very masculine smile. He pounded into her body as sweat covered his broad chest and dotted his face. Strain filled his expression and his breaths came in fast, ragged pants. He grunted with his efforts, drawing out her own frantic need, making her moan as well.

"More. More!" she cried out, bucking under him.

"Oh God!" he bellowed, continuing to grind mercilessly into her. "Uhhhhhh!" He erupted inside her as her body milked him for all he had.

She cried out as the last of his orgasm filled her. "Jason! Oh, Jason!" And then he collapsed on top of her and she held him to her.

* * * *

The rest of the week had passed in a blur. Jason pulled into the garage just after sundown. He sat in his truck for a second. He was tired. There had been party after party to make an appearance at. Between all of the socializing and his work around the ranch, he hadn't had the energy to even consider making love to Jen again. How damn sad was that?

He yawned, felt weariness weighing him down. He'd existed these last busy days on memories of that last special day with her. She'd let him do so much to her. He couldn't imagine any of the other women they knew putting up with his kinky demands at times. Yet he worried that maybe he'd gone too far, at least with suggesting they try another level of BDSM. The collar showing his ownership of her was only a small part of what he wanted. It would be a big step for her, though.

He thought about how she let him tie her up, make her walk around naked some days, paddle her, flog her. But she'd told him that the collar thing bothered her more than anything else. Something about it being the final act of losing herself, losing her independence.

Yes and no, in his opinion. He wanted to control her, own her because he loved her. He didn't want to destroy her. She needed to come to terms with what he wanted and with what he knew she could give. He'd seen her desire to let go, her enjoyment of what they did in her expressive eyes at times. He just had to keep nudging her toward the path he was certain would satisfy them both.

Time to go find her. He needed to see her sweet face. She had a way of settling him just by being near him. He walked into the house, still worrying about the thoughts that had played in his head all day. He needed to sit down and get her to talk to him. Even if he felt almost positive that she would adjust to a more intense lifestyle, being his slave, he would listen to her concerns. If she were really against even trying, he would give up the idea. But if she really wanted to stop what they'd been doing, he'd have a hard time dealing with that. He enjoyed their games. He believed she did as well.

Yet she'd become strangely quiet these last few days when they hadn't had time to play. That worried him. They definitely needed to talk.

The warmth felt good after coming in out of the cold, blustery day. He smelled chili and smiled. Maybe it wasn't your usual Christmas Eve dinner, but it was his favorite. Hot and spicy, with thick chunks of beef. She would have made cornbread, too. His stomach growled in anticipation.

"I'm in here," she called as he tugged off his coat and hung it in the mudroom. He toed off his boots and hung his hat on another wall peg. Then he went in search of the woman he loved.

Jennifer sat in front of the brightly lit tree waiting anxiously. Jason was finally home. Her heart raced. She had been waiting all day for him to get done with his chores. She'd wanted to start their traditional Christmas Eve time together early. It hadn't worked out. A couple of cattle had gotten out. He and the only two ranch hands still here at the ranch instead of somewhere with their families had had to track them down.

She heard him moving slowly through the mudroom, then the kitchen. Anticipation was killing her. She'd spent extra time making sure everything was perfect. She'd changed the sheets on the bed and added the new red, soft leather tethers she'd gotten, to surprise him with, to the four posts. Just in case. Then she'd made his favorite meal, something that could be eaten at any time...even put away until tomorrow, if that was the way the night went. She hoped it would.

"Smells good, sweetheart," he said and stepped into the family room. His eyes found her where she sat. "Well, hell! I should have let those damn cattle go. Should have come home a lot earlier."

The heat in his gaze as he looked at her went a long way toward easing her concerns. She'd worried about what she'd bought him for Christmas. This whole lifestyle was still new to her, but she was trying her best to make it work. For him. For them. From time to time he'd mentioned some things that interested him. It had taken her a while to wrap her head around it all. She'd been raised pretty conservatively. Yet gradually she'd started getting excited about trying some of the things that excited him. She just hoped she'd made the right decision.

He sucked in a deep breath making his big chest rise and fall in a shudder. His nostrils flared in obvious desire. He walked slowly forward, seeming unable to speak.

Don't move. Stay seated. She'd read some about how a submissive was supposed to behave. She had read about slave behavior, too, but she wasn't sure about that yet. Baby steps, she'd told herself. She would move forward slowly with this. The idea of him wanting to do this 24/7 still worried her, but she was willing to try.

"Merry Christmas," she said warily.

She felt awkward sitting here on this big red pillow, naked except for a wide red satin ribbon she'd managed to wrap around her and tie into a bow just above her breasts. What was he thinking? She wished he would say something.

As he moved closer, she saw the heat in his eyes. Warmth spread through her as well. She wanted to rub at her nervous stomach, yet she held still, waiting.

He stood looking down at her, breathing shallowly. "This is a sight I don't think I'll ever forget. Don't want to forget."

"There's more." Nerves fluttered in her abdomen. *Keep going. You can do this.* She nodded toward a box at her side. "Open it."

He seemed to have trouble looking away from her, but finally reached for the box. Impatiently, he tore the wrapping off and removed the lid. His eyes widened. "Really? You're okay with this?"

She hadn't been completely sure until the way he looked at her with such pride, such delight…such love. "I bought them because I trust you." She met his gaze. "Because I love you with all my heart."

She sat perfectly still as he pulled out the black leather collar, the word *submissive* imprinted on the front. He leaned down as she lifted her hair so that he could put it on. After snapping it in place, he gently cupped her face. "Thank you."

The emotion in his eyes, the tenderness in his voice, made her smile.

He reached again into the box he'd set down. He held up the nipple clamps with dangly strings of small silver stars. But he didn't move toward her with them. Instead he said, "We'll try these another time. I want to ease you into this stuff. Today the collar is enough." He choked up, cleared his throat. "Thank you."

Jason couldn't believe what she'd done for him. He'd seen her sitting there in a somewhat submissive slave manner and been surprised.

She was making an effort to tell him that she was willing to move their lifestyle to the next level. She hadn't exactly said that, but he understood. This was a huge step for her. Until now he'd bought everything they used in their games. Each time he'd worried that maybe he'd gone too far, but she'd never really complained. But this! A submissive's collar... nipple clamps. The collar represented something of big importance to her. He knew she saw it as losing who she was. He saw it as her trusting him enough to let him be in charge. He would never let her lose the very special woman she was. He would guard and protect her, own her...but with the strength of his love for her.

He looked down at the most precious gift from her, herself wrapped in a big red bow. When he'd seen her, his heart had nearly pounded right out of his chest. Never, ever would he forget this Christmas. He wanted to see her completely naked. Yet he was reluctant to remove the bow.

He thought about what he'd bought her and felt depressed. She'd probably like the necklace, but it was nothing compared to what she'd given him. He shifted around her and reached for the small box. "I'll get you something better. I promise."

She took the box with a gentle smile. "It's not the gift that matters. It's the thought behind it." She pulled off the wrapping. "I know how much you hate anything to do with shopping. But you love me enough to do it."

He waited nervously for her to look inside the box. He'd actually spent over an hour in the jewelry store making a decision. Every female salesclerk in there had taken pity on him, given him their advice. But he'd spotted this necklace on first entering the store and kept going back to it. *This* was the only one that came anywhere close to how he felt about Jen.

Her hands shook as she lifted the delicate silver strand from the box. He watched her carefully finger the intertwined silver hearts dotted with tiny diamonds. When she looked up at him, tears rolled down her cheeks. Her smile told him everything: she loved it.

"It's beautiful. Perfect." She climbed gracefully to her feet and moved into his embrace. The ribbon crinkling as she snuggled to him. "I love you so much."

He held her close, never wanting to let her go. She was the best gift he could ever get.

Naughty, Naughty Cowgirl

She was never going through another week like this one, not even another day. Her ass hurt from the second sound spanking in four days. Her heart hurt even more. How could she love Justin so much and dislike him at the same time?

Nicole walked gingerly from the kitchen toward the bedroom. She'd no sooner put the last of the Thanksgiving dinner dishes in the dishwasher after the last of their guests had finally left than Justin had turned on her. Okay, she'd been a little testy today. She was tired. Cooking for two days and getting the house sparkling clean for her in-laws, who didn't seem to like her that much, put her in a mood. Then they'd all but ignored her in the spirited table conversations about the ranch, a family reunion his mother wanted to have next summer, about... Well, about anything other than what she wanted or could talk about.

"No TV either," Justin called after her. "Straight to bed."

Straight to bed. You've been such a naughty girl today. I'm ashamed of your behavior. Yada, yada, yada. She was tired of being treated like a child. They'd been married over five years now. He needed to accept her for who she was.

She reached back to rub her stinging bottom. First thing tomorrow she was going to break every wooden spoon in the kitchen. Toss them in the trash. Maybe she had agreed to domestic discipline when they'd gotten married, but she hadn't really thought he would hold to the idea. At least not this long. From what he'd said when she'd grudgingly put the spoon in his hand and complained about getting another spanking, she would *never* be too old to go over his knee. Ha! She was already too old for this nonsense. It was time she made that clear to him.

"Did you hear me?"

Well, maybe she'd make a stand tomorrow about her decision. No sense risking another round with his hand blasting her sore bottom. "Yes. Straight to bed." She gave him the answer he wanted, but it didn't mean she had to like it.

She walked into the large master bedroom and stood in the doorway for a second. Justin had designed the log home and helped build it during their year-long engagement. She'd told him about things that she wanted in the house: a fireplace for the great room with a carved mantle like she'd seen in Branson, large windows to overlook the ranch yard, a kitchen with restaurant-style appliances because she loved to cook, a room for her painting studio, a hot tub on the deck for the two of them, a walk-in closet in the bedroom, and a big bay window with a seat there as well so she could sit and read sometimes. He'd given her all of it and so much more. He was a good man, a good husband...an amazing lover.

She heard him moving around in the kitchen, opening the refrigerator door, probably grabbing a beer. He liked drinking a beer when he watched football and he planned to watch the game tonight. If his parents and two brothers and their wives hadn't left, they might have stayed to watch the game with him. She'd not encouraged them to stay. Her behavior was complicated, but she'd reached her limit for tolerating them today.

Just once she would have liked to see her husband realize how awkward things were between her and his family. The man was sharp as a tack most of the time, except with anything to do with relationship things, touchy-feely stuff, then he was lost. Totally clueless.

With a sigh of frustration, she closed the door behind her and tossed her jeans and panties on the bench running along the end of the bed. At least he'd made her take them off and hadn't insisted she put them back on after he'd roasted her butt. Walking alone had been tough enough, with fabric rubbing her tender skin it would have been much worse.

She pulled off her T-shirt and bra to add to the small pile of clothes. As she turned, she glanced at the mirror over the dresser. No wonder her bottom felt like she'd been stung by a swarm of bees! There was hardly a square inch that wasn't bright red. He'd sure done the job this time. But then it hadn't helped her any when she'd reached back, somehow managed to grab hold of the spoon, and then whacked one of his shins with it before he snagged it back from her. Bad move on her part.

What was she going to do about this situation? She wanted to be married to Justin. Most of the time he was her true "other half." They could finish each other's sentences, knew what the other wanted at times. But there were also times when he stepped into his head of the household role and took it too seriously. He thought he knew what she needed, meaning some manner of spanking, to fix a misbehavior problem. Sort of his "easy way out" of dealing with a problem. She would have preferred talking it out...maybe heatedly discussing whatever it was. Like this time...the issues she had with his family. Maybe it would have led to more problems between them, maybe not. Done deal now, though. What she knew was that this would be the *last* spanking he'd give her!

Justin settled into the leather recliner and flicked on the TV. He took a swig of beer and set the bottle on the end table next to his chair. There was nothing better than watching football on Thanksgiving night. Except watching it with his dad and brothers.

He located the game with the remote and scowled. He'd be watching the game by himself this year and it pissed him off. Nicci had been a royal brat today. She'd acted strange from the moment his mother and sisters-in-law had come out of the kitchen after offering to help her. His mother had said his wife had everything under control, but he'd heard the underlying hurt in her tone. His sisters-in-law weren't usually big on helping out anyway and appeared to be relieved. When he'd gone into the kitchen to ask her about the situation, she had given him a wounded look, and then the usual, "Everything's fine" line.

His attention shifted to the TV but quickly back to his thoughts. What was going on with her lately? She'd started getting cranky earlier this week, grumbling around about all the cooking she needed to do for today. He'd even had to burn her ass a couple of days ago because she was having a meltdown. She'd been okay since then, until today. She'd avoided being around his family as much as possible; including insisting that she could finish the meal preparation by herself. She had hidden in the kitchen as long as she could, and then she hadn't said more than two words at the dinner table.

He frowned, puzzled by her behavior. It wasn't like her to be so rude. Her sour attitude had continued when they had started talking about a family reunion. She had clammed up even more, appearing to withdraw further into herself. Except he remembered her muttering something about being too busy even though they hadn't actually set a date. What was that about? Too busy? Finally the conversation had faded off, everyone tense. His family had decided it was best if they left right after the meal. Which was why he was here about to watch football alone, dammit.

He took another swig of beer, listening to the dishwasher in the other room. Not ten minutes ago he'd grabbed a thick wooden spoon from the ceramic utensil holder on the counter and his wife by her arm. He'd dragged her with him to the small table in the nook, sat down, and bent her over his knee. He'd wasted no time in giving her a couple dozen quick licks. She'd caught hold of the spoon and hit his shin with it, cussing at him. He'd regained control of the spoon and firmly showed her what an error she'd made. She wouldn't be trying that kind of nonsense again.

The commercial drew his attention for a second, but his focus quickly returned to his wife. Something was wrong between them. Something that had been growing for a while now. He didn't know what he'd done, but he sensed it was bad. He'd avoided actually asking her what was bothering her, hoping whatever it was would just fade away. Stupid, yes.

Maybe he should go to their room and try to make his way through that minefield of talking about emotions, feelings. Scary stuff, that. He was a guy; he didn't talk about feelings. One small misstep and he could make the problem worse. If it could get worse.

No. He'd stay here and watch the game. He'd sent her to bed early as part of the punishment, also to let her calm down. Hopefully, she would get beyond whatever had made her a crazy woman today. Later he'd go up and snuggle with her, maybe entice her into having sex with him. They hadn't made passionate love in a while now. Quick little comings together for satisfying their base needs, yes. But actually spending time and enjoying each other, no. He missed that. Maybe he was at fault. He just didn't know.

* * * *

Nicci watched Justin stomp into his boots and her heart felt heavy. He'd come to bed late last night, ready to make up with her. She'd tried to evade his attempts to pull her against him at first. But he could be very persuasive when he set his mind to loving her. And, boy, could her cowboy make love! She hadn't resisted that hard.

Well sated from last night and another round of heart-pumping, yes-yes-yes sex not long ago, she didn't have the energy to move yet. Besides, she wanted to savor every very fine inch of her handsome husband. She didn't want to forget anything about him. Not the dark hair that brushed his collar because he needed a haircut. Not the thick eyebrows that pulled together when he was upset or worried. Or the long nose with the slight bend from a scuffle with one of his brothers when they'd been teenagers. Certainly she wouldn't forget the sexy way he had of smiling crookedly at her when they made love. The list of what she loved about his physical appearance could go on and on. And there was a lot about him beyond looks that she loved. Yet she'd made a tough decision before he'd come up to bed last night and she was sticking to it.

"Are you going to work on those paintings for your show next month?" he asked, glancing back at her from the doorway.

He was late heading out for his share of the chores, late because he'd taken the time to do some extra fun and games with her. He'd seemed almost desperate to take her to the heights of pleasure this morning. She'd let him, knowing it might not happen again. Sadness weighed her down.

She scooted back against the headboard, pulling the sheet up to her bare breasts. She tried not to see the catch in his breath as he reacted to the glimpse of her naked body. How easily the man could get turned on sometimes. *Courage. Don't drag this out. Tell him.*

"No, I won't be painting today." She sucked in a steely breath. "I'll be packing."

Those eyebrows pulled together and his deep blue eyes narrowed. "Packing?"

She swallowed hard, twice. Could she really do this? Then before she could change her mind, she gushed out, "I'm moving into town."

He blinked in surprise and his shoulders stiffened beneath the blue plaid work shirt. "You're leaving me?" he asked grimly. His hands fisted at his sides, but he strangely remained calm otherwise.

"That's all you have to say? I announce that I'm moving out and that's it?" Pain pinched her heart. She could barely breathe. "No 'are you crazy?' or 'no way!'"

He appeared to struggle with what to say, opening his mouth

and then shutting it. His expression tightened. Finally he said, "I don't want you to go." His gaze met hers and she saw the pain in his eyes. "But I want you to be happy."

She almost changed her mind. Instead she fought to keep from crying and to keep from getting up to fling herself into his arms. She ached for him to just hold her. "Things haven't been right between us for some time now."

"I know," he admitted, sounding worried. "But I don't know what the hell to do about it. Because I don't know what I did wrong." He looked so frustrated, so lost.

Then he frowned. "Is it because I burned your ass yesterday? Because you think you're too old for disciplining?"

"That's part of it." She didn't like the discipline side of their marriage. He seemed to think that spanking solved problems instead of taking the time to talk about them. Verbal communication wasn't his best thing, at least not with her.

But there was more that bothered her than his failure to communicate with her or his quick decision to spank her instead of talking with her. He'd started hanging out more and more with some of his single ranching friends, going to play pool with them on Friday nights, or playing poker on Saturday nights. She'd been busy getting ready for her second art showing next month for the Christmas season. Yet she would have liked to go to a movie or out dancing with him like they used to do…if he'd asked. He hadn't. And she hadn't suggested it. Maybe she hadn't cared enough.

He swiped a hand through his hair as he often did when frustrated. "You knew my beliefs on the matter before we got married." He blew out a deep breath, his whole chest moving with it. "I suppose I can try to change. Stop spanking you."

Would that be enough? And was it fair of him to change part of who he was if she wasn't willing to change something as well? But she didn't know what about her to change. Not that she was perfect.

"I'm not saying I want a divorce, Justin. I just think we need some time apart. See what each of us really wants." Tears slipped down her face, her lower lip wobbled. Everything inside her felt tight and painful. She could still stop this, change her mind.

If she did stay, nothing would change. They'd continue along this growing farther apart path they'd started on. It wasn't good for either of them. For him to suddenly give up the spanking-man side of him wasn't enough. And her caving in on the matter wouldn't help their situation, either.

He straightened, his broad shoulders rigid. "Were you thinking about leaving me all the time we made love?"

She couldn't deny that it had been in her thoughts since last night. Her lips trembled. "Not all the time," she whispered. "I do love you." She did.

Hurt flashed in his eyes, echoed in his tone. "I can't help you move out. I just can't. But one of the men can help you when you're ready to go." He turned away, stopping with his back to her. "At least let me know before you leave."

How could she do this? How could she make love with him and then turn around and want to walk away? Justin walked in a dazed fog through the house. He felt shattered. He'd known something was wrong between them. But for her to leave him? It was worse than he'd imagined. How could he let her go? How could he not?

He stopped in the entry, reached for his coat, and strained to listen for sounds of his wife coming after him. He hoped with all his heart that she'd come flying down the hall to tell him she'd changed her mind.

But she didn't come. All he heard was the muffled sound of her crying. Even though leaving was her decision, clearly it wasn't easy for her. This was upsetting her as much as it was him.

Tugging on the coat, he battled down the desire to go back to her and beg her to stay. He could stop disciplining her, although it was something he truly believed in. Not hurting her, just helping her with some behavior issues she had sometimes. He hadn't understood that she was really against it. She'd never said as much, other than she felt she was too old to be spanked. But what woman didn't say that when she was about to get her butt roasted?

He snagged his hat from a hook and planted it on his head. Still, he didn't think her occasional trips over his knee were the real problem. He should go back and face her about what was going on in her head. Maybe if he understood how she felt… But after her shocking announcement to leave him, his own emotions were irrational right now. He was afraid he would push her too far, make it worse, if that was possible.

His stomach knotted with unease. He didn't want to lose the only woman he would ever love. She'd been so young, only nineteen, when they'd married. She'd dated some, but they'd fallen head-first in love almost from the moment they'd met. At least he had. She'd told him that she had, too, but maybe she hadn't really. That didn't matter. They'd been happy together…at least he'd thought they had.

He rubbed at the headache now adding to his misery. Maybe she'd matured enough now to realize she might have missed something before getting married. Maybe she needed more independence, although he thought he gave it to her. He watched over her, yes, tried to guide her, protect her, and support her. She had a mind of her own and he liked that. But at times she had problems with being too stubborn, with keeping things from him…like whatever was going on between her and his family. He needed to deal with that, but not today.

For now, he had to let her do what she thought was necessary. He had a feeling if he tried to stop her from leaving, he might really lose her. He had to let her go, had to figure out a way to make it right with her. He would, God help him.

＊＊＊＊

Nicole sat across from her sisters-in-law in Stanford's only real restaurant. Since it was the middle of the morning and snow was starting to fall there weren't many other customers. She hadn't seen either Janet or Wendy since Thanksgiving two weeks ago, but they'd come to the small house she'd rented a short while ago. They'd insisted she come get coffee with them and they hadn't taken "no" for an answer.

Janet, the older of the two and the one she'd never talked a lot with because she lived in Denver, looked at her with determination. "This is an intervention."

She'd been afraid of that. "Justin and I can deal with this ourselves." But they hadn't. Each of them had kept their distance.

"You aren't, though." Wendy, the petite blonde former cheerleader she'd known in high school, shook her head. "Your separation from Justin has the whole family worried."

"I doubt that, certainly not his parents." She fiddled with the rolled up silverware next to her. "His mother has never thought I was good enough for her oldest son."

"That's not true at all," Janet protested. She met Nicole's gaze when she looked up. "She's always worried that *he* didn't deserve *you*. You put up with his moods—and Lord knows he can be moody. We've all witnessed that. You have turned that scrappy old bachelor into a good husband. You—"

Nicole gaped at her, stunned by what Janet had said about her mother-in-law. At the same time she felt defensive about her husband. "I'm moody, too. He's patient with me, especially when I need to take time away from my wifely role to work on my painting."

"Wifely role?" Wendy raised a neatly plucked eyebrow in confusion.

"Cooking, cleaning. All that stuff."

"What about," Janet leaned closer, "sex? Is that the problem between you two? Is he…"

"No! At least not all of the time." She didn't want to talk about their sex life with her sisters-in-law. "We've just…I don't know…been drifting apart." Her cheeks heated but she looked from one woman to the other. "He's amazing when he puts his mind to it."

Janet and Wendy smiled at one another. "Like his brothers."

Then Wendy lowered her voice, "Is it the spanking thing, then?"

She sat back, shocked. "You know he spanks me? That it makes me feel like a naughty child?"

"We could only guess. Justin would never tell us about that personal kind of thing." Janet looked around and when it was clear nobody was listening to them, she continued. "The Phillips men are into that whole head of the household thing. A misbehaving woman—in their opinion—is going to get her bottom warmed."

"Both of you…" She couldn't finish the question, it seemed too crazy.

The women bobbed their heads. "Not any fun, but I know Bob loves me," Janet said.

"Same with Alan," Wendy added.

"Is Justin really that unreasonable about it? Has he hurt you?" Janet pressed.

"No, but I don't like it." Yes, he'd started spanking her more often lately. But then she'd gotten pretty testy, too, with the pressures of the holidays and her showing coming up. It was annoying to have to suffer a sore bottom and go about her business too.

Janet snorted. "What woman does?"

Wendy's face grew pink. "Well…when you get spanked in foreplay…"

Nicole and Janet both gaped at her. Nicole remembered Justin mentioning such a thing once, but they'd never done it. Her spankings were all serious.

"Do you love him?" Janet asked.

"Yes." That hadn't changed. She cried herself to sleep every night. She thought about him all day as she tried to paint. But she hadn't called him. And he hadn't called her. "But I'm not sure how he feels."

Wendy's eyes widened. "Are you serious? The man is crazy in love with you, has been from the first time he met you. He built that fancy house with everything you mentioned. Even added more details he thought you'd like, like that over-sized tub in your bathroom."

"He's grumpier than an old bear, according to his brothers, who hear about it from his ranch hands. He doesn't sleep, doesn't eat." Janet told her, shaking her head sadly. "But he's determined to let you make whatever decision you need to. He's determined to find a way to live with it."

Not sleeping. Not eating. Miserable too. Nicole felt worse than ever. She was making them both miserable. But she was done with this, or would be after she got through her exhibit next week in Denver.

* * * *

Hope had lit inside Justin when he'd gotten a voice mail from Nicci out of the blue. She was in Denver at her showing and would be coming back to Stanford right before Christmas. She hadn't actually said she was coming here, but he was praying she would. God, he missed her.

He studied the tree he'd had one of his men help drag in earlier. He should have gone to her showing, but he'd been so depressed he hadn't wanted to ruin her big moment. So he'd stayed at the ranch and moped around. Actually he'd moped around ever since she'd driven away almost a month ago. Why the hell hadn't he called her?

Because he hadn't wanted to hear her say she wanted a divorce. Because communication wasn't something he was good at. Somehow he needed to get better at it. He didn't have time for a course on it and he wasn't great at reading books, either. Maybe he should see a therapist, a marriage counselor. Maybe *they* should see one together.

His gaze shifted to the stack of boxes with decorations he'd dragged down from the attic. He usually helped with this, but she was in charge of decorating the tree and house. He wasn't even sure he could do this on his own, or whether he wanted to.

Just as he was about to sit in his chair and give it more thought, he spotted three cars pulling into the driveway. He hadn't talked to any of his family since Thanksgiving, except over the phone. Now they were all here. His mother, his dad, his sisters-in law Wendy and Janet, his brothers, Bob and Alan.

As the car doors opened, he noted that even his four nieces and nephews were about to invade his home. He wasn't sure exactly how he felt about their presence, especially his mother's. He'd come to realize that she had a lot to do with his wife's unhappiness and attitude problem on Thanksgiving, although he wasn't sure how she figured into the equation. What he knew was that he was slow in figuring stuff like that out.

He opened the front door even before one of them could ring the doorbell. His mother looked straight up at him, her chin thrust out, determined. "We've come to help put up your decorations. For sweet Nicole."

"She's not here." He was afraid to even think that she might not ever be here again.

"She will be, though. You have to have faith." His mother swept by him, shedding her coat and handing it to him. "I want your home to be perfect when she comes. She loves Christmas so much."

"Mom, did you say something to my wife that..." He wasn't sure how to ask if she'd in some way hurt Nicci.

The rest of the family had started walking inside, taking off coats and boots. One after the other moved around them and into the great room, heading for the many boxes. But his mother waited until they were alone again before she said, "It's more what I *didn't* say, son. But I'll make peace with our Nicole. I promise."

She started to turn away, then faced him again. Her expression was stern. "You need to fix this."

"But I—"

"No excuses. This is too important, Justin. You need to talk out your problems." She blew out a breath and glanced toward his father by the doorway. "I realize you didn't inherit a touchy-feely gene from your father. But even your father and I have figured out that sometimes we just need to discuss issues...even argue on occasion."

He watched her walk away, feeling chastised. She was right. Their marriage was the most important thing in his world. He would have to deal with saving it.

* * * *

Nicole turned onto the road leading to the ranch yard. Christmas Eve day. She was upset with herself for staying in Denver so long. Her showing had gone well and she'd sold almost every painting. But one of the patrons who had bought three of her Western landscapes had wanted to hire her to do more for several of his offices. He'd insisted she stay an extra day to visit those offices and see what would work best in each of them. That was great, of course, but she'd been anxious to get back to Justin.

She stopped the car, looked toward the house, and saw lights running across the front porch and over the garage. They were on even though it was only mid-day. They'd never put up outside lights before, but she liked the idea. Had he put up their Christmas tree as well? She hoped so, yet she felt bad about not being here to help with that. They'd always done it together.

Knots tied and re-tied in her stomach. Nerves tingled in her abdomen. Her heart raced, in anticipation…in dread…in worry. What if she'd ruined everything by moving out? What if he couldn't fully love her again? She'd panicked under all the pressure she'd felt lately. It really hadn't been because he'd taken that awful spoon to her bottom. Sure it had hurt and bruised her pride, too. And she still planned to get rid of every wooden spoon in the kitchen.

Her cell phone buzzed in her purse on the passenger seat. Jarred back to the moment, she reached for it. Before she could even answer she heard Justin's deep voice say, "Are you going to sit there all day?"

He sounded wary; like he was afraid she would turn around and drive away. Those tingles she'd felt in her abdomen spread lower. Her body recognized her lover's voice, wanted him.

"Will you let me in?" She asked the question she'd been worrying about. What if he'd had enough of her? What if she'd stayed gone too long?

"If you don't get in here soon, I'm coming out to haul you in here." Now he sounded determined, although there was still a hint of concern in his tone.

"Oh, Justin…" She broke into sobs. "I don't deserve you."

It took him a second before he said in a husky tone, "Wrong, sweetheart. It's *I* who doesn't deserve you." He pulled in a breath. "Now get your sweet ass in here. I need you. Always."

Her sweet ass. She was pretty sure he wasn't talking about wanting to spank her, even if he might think she had earned it for running away instead of staying to discuss their issues together. She'd accepted the kind of man he was when they'd been dating. She wouldn't always go willingly over his knee, but she wasn't refusing to acknowledge that need in him to be the head of their household. He wasn't the kind of man who easily talked about feelings, none of the men in his family did.

She'd have to be the leader in that department. They'd have to compromise in some areas, learn better how to communicate with each other. While they'd been separated, she'd realized that she needed to stand her ground with him more. He wasn't an ogre by any means and she wasn't scared of him. She'd have to help him understand her better. And, hopefully, there would be fewer and fewer times when he believed it necessary to take her over his knee. But that was a minor issue, as far as she was concerned.

"I bought something for you." She squirmed on the seat, thinking about what she wore beneath the knee-length coat. "Actually, several things."

"All I want is *you* for Christmas, darlin'. That's more than enough." He disconnected, but she'd heard the strength of emotion in his voice. She didn't doubt for a second that he still loved her.

* * * *

She was home. *Thank God.* Justin stood at the big front window and watched his precious wife stop in the driveway. He hurried to the garage as the door creaked open. He wasn't sure when he'd ever felt this anxious. Never before had things mattered this much. He'd better damn well not screw this up. Which were pretty much the words his mother had said to him before they'd left the other day. His dad hadn't said anything, but the look he'd given Justin as he left had said as much.

As she opened the car door, he struggled to wait for her. But when she glanced at him and he saw tears on her face, saw the hesitancy in her expression, he strode toward her.

"You're so beautiful." He hugged her to him, felt her shivering in his hold. "I need you so much."

To his relief, she moved closer in his embrace, rubbed against his obvious erection. "I need you, too."

He kissed the top of her head, drew in the strawberry scent of her shampoo. "I *need* you *that* way, yes." He eased back to meet her eyes. "But I need you for a lot more than that. This house was so empty without you here."

She gave him a final hug and dashed away the tears. Giving him a cautious smile, she headed for the trunk. "I'll need your help with one of your gifts."

He noticed her cheeks turning pink and wondered what that was about. But when the trunk opened and he saw a strange looking bench with what looked like some kind of restraints by the front legs, he cocked his head. "What's this?" Surely it wasn't...

She couldn't meet his eyes as she reached inside for the two wrapped boxes next to the bench. "It's, ummm...a discipline bench."

His mouth fell open. *What the hell?* "You're kidding me." How did she even know about that kind of thing?

"I know it's sort of strange. Me buying this." She glanced at him and away again. "I'm just trying to tell you that..." She swallowed hard, blushed, and said awkwardly, "Well, that I'm all right with your need for discipline."

She raised her gaze. "At least to a limited extent." She worried her lip, then added, "Maybe we could...well...explore other things. Like sensual spankings. Maybe some kind of kinky play."

"Hell, darlin'," he said stunned. "I'd been willing to give up the whole punishment thing. Anything to have you back."

She blinked at him, smiled, and waited for him to say more.

Words weren't his friend at the best of times. Getting them out was damn hard. But she'd brought him this special gift, which still shocked the hell out of him. He felt humbled and intrigued by her and the possibilities this presented.

He reached inside to lift it out, studying the angled bench with its two padded places. One longer area obviously for her to stretch face down over, another for her knees to rest on. It was clear her sweet little butt would be thrust into a very vulnerable position. And its use wasn't limited to punishment and lighting a fire to her ass. His mind was already alive with visions of much more enjoyable things.

His jeans suddenly felt tight. "Let's take this inside. I've got an idea I want to try out."

She looked up at him, paler now, worrying her pretty lower lip. "Okay."

He set the bench down, shut the trunk, and said gently, "No, darlin', I'm not intending what you're clearly thinking. I have something else in mind. Something I think we'll both really enjoy."

"This doesn't mean—"

"I know," he interrupted. "Just because you brought some kind of peace offering doesn't mean everything is fine. You wouldn't have left in the first place without good reason." He touched her face and said intently, "We'll figure things out. I promise. Just give me a chance, that's all I ask."

She turned her head to kiss his palm. "I'm as much at fault as you are. But we'll talk later." She nodded to the bench. "I'm curious about what you mentioned, something we'll enjoy."

Nicole walked nervously into the house, clutching her other gifts. Had getting him this bench been the stupidest idea ever? She'd seen it in the specialty shop she'd gone to and thought it would be a big improvement over being bent over the bar stool, the table, the counter, any surface other than her husband's lap. As embarrassing as that was, she preferred feeling his hard thighs beneath her stomach. But this had nice padded surfaces for those other times.

She carried her boxes into the great room, thinking about the odd gleam in his eyes. What had he been considering? Something they would enjoy?

"Did we do okay?" he asked sounding anxious behind her.

"We?"

She glanced through teary eyes around the room. There was her collection of Santas all across the fireplace mantle, just as she usually put them. Her mother's Christmas afghan lie spread over the back of the sofa. Fake holly was draped over the curtain rod, again, like she usually put it. And he'd put up an even bigger tree than normal. All of their ornaments covered it, even some she hadn't put out in the last couple of years because she'd thought it was too much. He'd put *all* of them on the tree.

"It's all so beautiful," she whispered in awe.

"I wanted everything out in case you came home."

When she looked at him, he was blushing. It was so sweet that she sniffed back tears.

"My family showed up just as I was about to tackle the job myself," he explained before she could say anything.

His family helped him? Now she felt bad. *She* should have done this, with him. "I'm sorry for not being here."

"Doesn't matter…you're here now. That's what matters." He walked around her to set the bench down in front of the tree. "I'd kind of like to try out my idea, if you're game."

Suddenly she felt awkward about the bench thing, but he looked so hopeful and sexy. His gaze had darkened. Her heart pounded and warmth spread through her.

She set her boxes to the side for later and then unbuttoned her coat. Her stomach once more fluttered with nerves as she eased the coat off and let it pool at her feet. She'd seen these skimpy little panties and barely-there bra in Shandra's Secrets at the mall in Denver and decided to be bold. Her husband was a pretty conservative guy, but she'd imagined he might like the outfit. Hoped he would.

His eyes had widened in obvious admiration. He was breathing hard. And when she looked lower, she noted that an erection pushed at the front of his jeans. Everything in her tingled in awareness. Want. She wanted him so bad.

Since he appeared unable to function or speak, she took a chance on what he'd been thinking about. She moved to the bench, faced away from him, and slowly wiggled the panties off, kicked off her shoes too. Then she stretched over the bench. It was kind of strange, but she could live with this. Her butt was definitely up in the air and would be in a very bad position—depending on your point of view.

He sucked in a shuddery breath and then he began tearing off his clothes. She trembled, waited, uncertain exactly what to expect.

He moved behind her, smoothed his hand over her bare bottom, making it quiver. "Let me go grab some lube. Stay right here."

Lube. She was already so wet and ready… *Oh!* He wanted to… *Oh.* It had been a long time since they'd done this, but she tingled in anticipation.

A few minutes later as Justin finally was fully inside her tight hole, she relaxed over the bench. She'd been glad he'd decided to fasten the restraints over her wrists, glad she could clamp her hands around the bench legs. It had taken a lot of lube and some gentle working with his fingers before she could accept his long, thick rod. They'd both had some heavy-breathing moments.

He held still, letting her adjust and catch her breath. His big hands gently caressed her back, her ass cheeks. "Thank you," he said quietly.

She felt him so deep inside her. It was odd, but it no longer stung. She even managed to press back against him. "For the bench? For letting you take me this way?"

He rocked carefully back and forth, making her shiver at the exquisite fullness. "For those things, too." He clasped her hips and pulled nearly out before sliding deep again. "For coming back to me."

Suddenly she knew what she really wanted...what they'd both been wanting. She craned her head to look back at him. The sight of him standing behind her, knowing he was driving into her ass, took her breath away for a second. Then she recovered and asked cautiously, "Could you shift to doggy style? I'm okay with you taking me from behind, but..."

"I worried that you wouldn't like this." He stopped moving, pulled out and she gave a small moan at the sudden emptiness. "I'll go get a condom."

"No!" she said abruptly. She met his puzzled gaze. "I don't really mind this and we can do it another time. But I want...let's work on making a baby."

She'd never seen him cry, even look weepy. Yet his eyes had appeared shiny when he'd walked up to her in the garage. Now he was blinking rapidly and grinning at the same time.

"You're sure? Even after I screwed up enough that you left me?"

"Like you said, we'll fix our problems. I have faith in you." She changed her mind and wiggled her bottom at him. "Change of plans. Let's stay right here. Think you can...ummm...try making a baby here?"

He didn't wait for a second invitation. She purred in happiness as he drove deep inside her. It felt amazing to be taken this way. "Oh, yes, I like this bench!" she purred.

He stood still, throbbing inside her. "Works for me, too."

As she lowered her head, she caught sight of the other gifts she had for him. Would she like him using the velvet flogger on her bare butt, too?

All I Want for Christmas (Biggest Prize Ever)

I love him. I love him not. I love him. Krystal twisted the stem on the apple, doing her own version of the plucking of petals in the time-honored tradition of determining if she loved Ryan Evans. Okay, so she cheated and pulled the stem out before it was ready to come out on its own.

She did love the bad-ass bull rider. The problem was so did most of the rodeo bunnies that hovered around him at each and every rodeo he rode in. She wasn't into sharing.

Handing the apple to Rebecca, she heaved a frustrated sigh. "What am I going to do about him? Yes, kicking him in the nuts when he comes home again is an option." In her mind's eye, she saw the latest photo on his website. He was grinning as always, with his arms around two gorgeous women after his last rodeo. She fought back tears stinging her eyes. "What happened to 'You're the *only* woman for me'? I'm pretty sure I didn't misunderstand those words he said the last time he was here."

The beloved Palomino he'd given her for Christmas last year chomped on the apple but remained otherwise silent. But then Rebecca adored Ryan…like every other female—no matter the species—on the darn planet. The problem was she loved him too. She didn't want to.

Her older brother, his best friend, had warned her against it. Her mother adored his charming side, but even she had cautioned her against a bad boy like him. And her dad…well, he'd sworn that if she started seeing Ryan again after he'd broken her heart this summer, he'd take the brush to her bottom like he'd done when she was a rebellious teenager.

She looked around the big, warm barn where her father housed his prized rodeo stock breeding horses during the winter. He was all gruff talk for the most part and she doubted he'd actually paddle her, but the idea did make her have second thoughts. Not that she intended on getting involved with Ryan again when he came home this week to see his folks for Thanksgiving. She might love him, but she wasn't stupid.

The large double door at the other end of the building slid open and a blast of cold air swept inside. She turned at the interruption and found her mother in the doorway. Even from here, she could see the worry on her mother's still unlined face. "There's a call for you on the main line. It's Ryan." She hesitated. "I can tell him..."

That you don't want to talk to him. Her mother's words went unsaid, but she understood them. She shook her head and moved toward the phone on the center post in the long aisle. It was one of the only land-lined phones remaining on the ranch. "I'll talk to him."

"I should have told him you weren't here."

"It's okay, Mom." As she picked up the phone, her mother gave her a regret-filled look and left the barn, closing the door behind her. Her mother was probably right that she shouldn't talk to him, but...

"Hello, Ryan," she kept her tone as casual as she could manage.

"Damn, darlin', it's good to hear your voice again." His familiar, sexy as hell rumble made her body purr in pleasure. It always had, or at least since she'd fallen in lust over him almost ten years ago, at sixteen. After being his lover off and on these last few years, her reactions to him were even stronger. She ached in places she shouldn't, desired him with every foolish fiber of her being.

She let his comment go. She was a bad judge of when he was serious anymore. The man was an easy-going flirt with any woman near him. It came natural to him, like breathing. "I heard you're coming to see your parents this week. Your mom has been cooking up a storm, making all of your favorites. According to what she's told my mother, that is."

"She's always determined to fatten me up." He sounded pleased and amused. "I can't wait to see them. You, too. Especially you."

She'd heard the change in his tone, the fading of amusement. If she hadn't seen the gazillion pictures of him with one pretty young woman after another plastered on every rodeo site she followed trying to keep up with him, she might have believed him. She really needed to get a handle on this obsession she had for him. It kept her comparing every man she dated to the handsome blond cowboy. Including Todd, the widowed banker she'd gone out with more than anyone else. Most of those she'd dated were solid men, settled in the community, would make great husbands and good fathers. But none of them were Ryan. *Pitiful. You're just pitiful.*

"I'm going to be pretty busy," she said flatly, hoping he didn't hear the sadness in her voice. She needed to be strong, resist him this time.

The problem was that they'd had good times together. He made her laugh, made her feel special. He saw beyond the simple second grade teacher she was, drew out the sensual woman inside her. But he'd never said anything about a future together. He never talked about anything but the next rodeo, nothing about his life after he stopped working the circuit. That line about her being "the only woman for him" had just been one of his lines to make a woman feel good. She was certain of it. After all, if he'd been serious, wouldn't he have kept in touch with her? Sent her an email once in a while? Facebooked her? He had a huge following, of which she—foolishly—was one.

He'd been quiet while her mind had wandered. Maybe he'd disconnected and she'd missed it. "Are you still there?"

"Yes, just thinking." He hesitated and then asked warily, "Are you upset with me?"

Maybe he wasn't quite as clueless as she'd thought. But she didn't want to get into a deep conversation, really any kind of conversation. "No. I just have a lot of things to do. Family dinner, of course, tomorrow. Papers to grade. School stuff." The school work was under control, but he didn't need to know that.

"Can't you squeeze in at least a little time for me? I'm only going to be here for a few days. I won't be home again until Christmas."

He sounded almost hurt, like he was begging. Odd. But she was wary of giving him an inch, fearing he'd grab for a foot. She'd learned the hard way that if you gave him what he wanted, he took it and more. Especially when it came to letting him have a simple kiss. Kissing him led to him stripping her before she had known what was happening. It had led to him laying her out and feasting on her—not that that had been a bad thing. He repeated all of it every time they were together because she couldn't resist him. Every time he left her totally boneless and so content she never wanted to move again. The man was DANGEROUS in big-time capital letters.

"Please, darlin'," he prodded. "I really need to see you." That really did sound like begging, which boosted her ego.

As always, she weakened. With a defeated sigh, she said, "I'll meet you at Sal's Pizza Place at noon on Friday. Take it or leave it." For clarification—for him? For her?—she added, "No sex this time. I mean it. Pizza or nothing."

"I'll be there." He hung up before she could chicken out and she wondered if he'd known she was considering just that.

* * * *

Ryan waited anxiously in a booth in Sal's Pizza Place in Middleton, Kansas. He hadn't been in here since high school but the place hadn't changed a bit. The tables scattered around were mismatched, as were the chairs. The clock on the far wall always seemed to be off, since Sal didn't get around to adjusting it to daylight savings time. His wife, Connie, had put on quite a few pounds but her attitude hadn't changed. She still mothered everyone who walked in the door. Including him.

"You need more meat on your bones," she said, sadly shaking her head at him. Then she followed his glance to the door. "Expecting someone?" She grinned in mischief. "Our sweet little Miss Krystal?"

He already knew everyone in town adored Krystal Carter. His mother always told him every detail about what was going on with her whenever he called home. She volunteered around town for anything that needed help. She sang in the church choir, "like an angel." But the latest news he'd received was that she'd been dating a lot this summer, particularly a widowed banker. A revelation he'd heard yesterday at Thanksgiving dinner. His mom had reluctantly told him the news and he'd felt sucker-punched. She was *his* girl! Evidently she didn't understand that, but he'd always thought it was a given.

The door opened and this time when he looked in that direction, he saw the woman he loved. His heart skipped a beat and he smiled in relief, the day already feeling better. He'd been worried that she might not come. He hadn't seen her since May, when he'd been in town for Mother's Day. Damn, he'd missed her.

She gave a weak smile and headed toward him. His stomach tightened; his palms were sweating. You'd think he was on his first date, worried about impressing her. He'd known Krystal all her life and known since she'd turned sixteen that some day she'd be his forever. Sure, she'd dated in high school and in college. They'd talked about it. He'd wanted her not to miss out on the dating experience. He hadn't liked her hanging out with other men, even if he hadn't led the life of a saint while working the rodeo circuit over the years. But he'd never gotten seriously involved with another woman. In his head and heart, he knew they would end up together. And she'd never shown any real interest in anyone besides him. So he'd been okay. Until now.

She'd thrown a kink in his plan by getting serious about another man. It was supposed to be him. Always *only* him.

"Hi, sweetie," Connie said and helped Krystal off with her coat. "I'll give you two a few minutes to decide what you want." She walked away, but not before she looked worriedly at him.

"Pretty as ever," he said, taking in everything about her as he always did. He meant it, too. There had never been a woman prettier, at least not in his biased opinion.

She'd let her chin-length hair grow out, now it fell in soft, warm auburn waves over her shoulders. Shoulders that appeared tense. Actually she looked stiff all over, distant. This was so unlike the way she usually reacted when they got together after being apart for a month or two. But he suddenly realized he hadn't seen or talked to her in six months. *Six months?* No wonder she was pissed at him. How the hell had he let so much time get by him?

She eased into the other seat and focused on folding her coat just right instead of looking at him. "Are you leaving tomorrow? Or this weekend?" She glanced at him and took the rolled-up silverware and started unrolling it.

Unable to help himself, he reached across the table and gently touched her hand. So soft, fragile, feminine.

She jerked it away, her eyes flashing fire at him.

"Honey, what's wrong? What did I do?" If he thought about it, he could probably come up with a hell of a long list.

"Hmmm, let me see...." She leaned back far enough he couldn't touch any part of her. "You tell me I'm the *only* woman in your life, then you forget about me. You flirt with every rodeo bunny that crosses your path."

"I do no such thing," he protested. At her raised voice, he glanced around the partially filled restaurant. Nobody was paying them any attention. Okay, maybe he flirted a bit, but he'd not done more than that. He'd been tempted many times. Some of those young women could be pretty insistent. "I didn't cheat on you."

She dared to roll her eyes at him. "Yeah, right. I've seen the pictures on your website and on your Facebook page. You out celebrating at some bar after yet another win."

"I don't lie." Damn his frequent rodeo-traveling companion. Toby was into all of that Internet stuff, not him. Toby had created both the website and the Facebook page for him. He'd hardly even looked at it. Social media wasn't his thing. But he knew there had been pictures taken many times. He never thought much about them. "They're only photos. Nothing more."

She gave an unladylike snort. Her eyes looked teary and she drew in a shaky breath. "You're a highly sexual man. I can't believe you've been celibate since the last time we were together."

That she thought so little of him bothered him, a lot. He might not be the best man around or even worthy of someone as smart as she was, but he didn't cheat. He'd made a commitment to her and he'd stood by it. Did she know he'd made a commitment to her? Had he actually said the words out loud? He thought he had, but maybe he hadn't. Still, she should have known he was serious.

He frowned. "Don't be like this, darlin'. Trust in me. I haven't changed. I'm still the same man you've known and loved."

She set the silverware aside and waved Connie away as she approached the table. As the older woman walked off, Krystal met his gaze. "That's the problem, Ryan. You've been an outrageous flirt ever since you were a teenager. You're a natural-born charmer. I've been charmed, too. But I need more than a man who is in and out of my life whenever he damn well pleases."

His stomach knotted just like it did when he climbed atop a bull. Fear always threatened to make him climb right back off, but he never did. He wasn't a man who gave up easily. And having her in his life was a hell of a lot more important than winning yet another buckle. It was time to take the next step in his life. He'd already discussed it with his folks, not about him getting married, but him settling down.

He sucked in a breath and looked straight at her. "I'm giving up the rodeo life. My last ride will be in December."

Her eyes widened and then doubt slid over her face. "Every time you've been injured you've said you were quitting. Then you heal up and go right back to the circuit."

"I wasn't ready, not really ready, before." He understood her reluctance to believe him and wasn't sure he could convince her he wanted a change. He'd clearly "called wolf" too many times already. "I mean it, darlin'. I'm coming back to start taking over the ranch. Mom and Dad want to retire to Florida. They need to. Dad's health won't let him keep on ranching much longer."

He thought about how different his dad had seemed yesterday. Arthritis had nearly crippled his hands and knees. Pain etched his thinning face. He was a proud man and the idea of no longer being able to work the ranch like he'd done all of his life was killing him. Ryan had to step in and be the man they needed him to be. And he needed to support his mom as she dealt with all of these changes. He *wanted* to be a responsible son, *wanted* to prove to them—and clearly to Krystal—that he was more than just a bull rider. Hell, he was getting too damn old for riding bulls anyway. He'd broken so many bones over the years that the doctors had told him he'd face having arthritis in his joints one day. He hoped that day was a long way off, but it would come.

Sadness replaced the irritation in her expression. She leaned closer and reached out for him, but then pulled her hand back. "I've known your dad's been having health problems. I just never... Well, I don't think any of us around here ever imagined him giving up the ranch. I'm sorry."

"Me too." He swallowed hard. Seeing his dad failing like that had been difficult. He closed his eyes for a second before looking at her again. "I need you, more than ever." He hesitated. "I've *always* needed you in my life."

She shook her head, wariness in her gaze. "I don't think that's true. I've always been there for you when you wandered back home for a few days. I've been your friend...and your lover...of convenience."

She blinked back tears and he could almost feel the hurt he saw in her eyes. "I can't go on like this anymore." She grabbed her coat and scooted out of the booth. "I'll be your friend, I could never stop being that. But I can't be your whenever-you-need-me lover anymore. I just can't."

"Krystal, please..." He let the plea fade away. Wrong place, wrong time. But he was *not* giving up on her. He couldn't.

He forced himself to stay put. It was hard not to grab her and pull her to him while she tugged on her coat. Then instead of walking off, she surprised him by leaning down and giving him a quick kiss. It shook him clear to his bones. God, how he'd needed that.

But his pleasure was short lived. Regret filled her eyes as she said in a trembling whisper, "Everyone has always warned me away from you. I never listened. Dad even told me the other day that he would take the brush to my bottom if I got involved with you again. He won't have to, because I'm not."

He looked steadily at her. "Maybe *I* should give you a spanking. For being so pig-headed stubborn and not believing in me."

She straightened to glower down at him. "You've done that a few times over the years. But trust me, cowboy, it's *never* happening again."

He watched her storm across the restaurant, watched the sweet sway of her hips in the skinny jeans. Damn but she had a great ass. He'd definitely be taking her over his knee again. There was nothing more in life he liked than a challenge. Now he faced a lot of them, but he was confident he could meet them all. Leaving the rodeo would be hard, but his body was more than ready. Taking over the ranch would be a definite trial, but he could do it. He'd always known he would one day and had even started thinking about some of the things he would do differently. The challenge that mattered most, though, was proving to Krystal that he could do all of this…and that he loved her with all of his heart.

* * * *

Krystal wandered through the mall with all of the other last minute shoppers. She should be home helping her mom get ready for the family Christmas breakfast tomorrow and then the chaotic gift exchange that followed. But she'd been an emotional basketcase ever since seeing Ryan after Thanksgiving. She shouldn't have agreed to meet him. She'd known how hard it would be to break up with him. Yes, that had been her intention…and she had…sort of. She hadn't counted on him being devastated by it since he seemed to have an endless number of women who chased after him.

I didn't cheat on you. Could she really believe him? Could she really trust him with her heart? Again. She'd promised to remain his friend, to support him however he needed her to, assuming he actually settled at the ranch. But could she be *only* his friend?

She knew his folks had already left for Florida. She usually spent Christmas Eve together with him and his parents. This year he would be alone for Christmas. The idea bothered her. He wasn't good at being alone.

I don't lie. She hugged her purse tighter to her side. She'd always trusted him before. But all of those pictures… *Believe him, at least give him the benefit of the doubt.* Her heart wasn't quite ready to completely give up on him.

She stepped to the side of the crazily rushing shoppers and found she'd stopped next to Ramona's Decadent Lingerie. She'd been in there dozens of times when she'd known he was coming home soon. He had a real fondness for sexy little panties and corsets. And she liked the way his eyes heated when he saw her, the way he spent serious time enjoying her, undressing her. Money always well spent. But his time for seeing her in such an outfit was in the past. *Right?*

A sexy little babydoll nightgown caught her attention. It was red, apron-style, with white fur trim and a matching thong. Perfect for Christmas. Ryan would freak out if he saw her in that, freak out in a deliciously *hot* way. Her body thrummed in anticipation.

Okay, she wanted him. And she wanted to believe him, trust in what she'd seen in his eyes when he'd started to plead with her not to give up on him. She'd thought over and over about that simple kiss. It had been simple and yet so complicated.

She stepped toward the doorway, heart racing. She had no business even thinking about the little Christmas lingerie item, absolutely shouldn't be considering going in to see if they had her size. Then almost before she had another sane thought, she was handing over her credit card at the checkout register.

She walked out of the store, bag in hand, and knew where she wanted to spend Christmas Eve, good or bad. She would go to him, share one more special time with him…but she'd pray it wouldn't be their last.

* * * *

He should have gone with his folks to Orlando instead of staying here in this big old house alone. The ranch hands could easily have handled everything until he got back in a week or so. But something had kept him from leaving. *Krystal.* He hadn't seen her since that awful day at the pizza place. He'd been so busy wrapping up what he needed to with his final ride, with his sponsors, and then dealing with the legal details about the ranch. She'd been in his thoughts, though, every minute of the day.

It felt like he had a hole in his chest, his heart ached with missing her. They usually spent Christmas Eve together with his parents. For years his mom and dad had looked at her as their "daughter." He knew his mom had always hoped he would get around to making her a permanent part of their family. She wanted her for a daughter-in-law. She'd been so disappointed when he'd reluctantly admitted that he'd screwed up and maybe lost her. But when he'd taken them to the airport in Kansas City, she'd taken him aside and firmly told him not to give up on her. She'd told him that Krystal loved him, had loved him for a long time.

He drew in a shaky breath, praying that his mom had been right. Now all he needed to do was scrape together the courage to go after Krystal and change her mind about him. Well, that, and he had to have a talk with her father. It was time they came to an understanding and time he earned the respect of the other man so important in her life.

Loneliness ate at him, but he couldn't go to the Carter's home now. This was family time and he wasn't part of their family. He'd have to wait until after Christmas. But he couldn't bear the idea of going to watch TV in the great room. His mom had left the decorated tree up and he didn't want to look at it again, knowing he'd miss his folks… and miss Krystal.

He began turning off the lights downstairs, deciding to go up to his room. Maybe he'd read a little. Maybe he'd…

As he put a foot on the stairs near the front door, he heard the crunch of tires on the gravel in front of the house. He couldn't imagine who it might be. He'd given all but one of the men today and tomorrow off and they'd gone to be with family. Curious, he went to the door and pulled it open.

His heart pounded and he stared in surprise at the sight of Krystal climbing out of her Mini Cooper. How many times had he teased her about the ridiculous little car? Now he was damn glad to see it.

He should have rushed out to meet her, should have scooped her into his arms and carried her into the house. Instead he called on every ounce of control he had left and waited for her to come to him. He was determined to win her back, but he was also worried about scaring her off again. It hurt that she'd believed he had bedded other women. Sure, he liked to flirt, but there had never been and never would be another woman for him. He'd looked at his website and felt sick. He'd never given those pictures much thought, until he saw them from her point of view. They were coming off that site ASAP!

She walked up the sidewalk, appearing uncertain. In the light from the porch he could see the worry in her eyes, saw the way she nibbled on her lower lip like she did whenever she was nervous. She stopped at the bottom of the porch steps. "Can I come in?"

Her sense of uncertainty got to him. All that mattered was she'd come to him. They had a lot to work through, but he'd worked damn hard to get to the top of the PBR, to be the best of the professional bull riders. He didn't give up when he had a goal in mind. He wanted her for his wife.

"Always," he said huskily. "You're *always* welcome here." He stepped aside so she could walk by him. As she did, he drew in her scent, something lightly minty this time. He liked it.

She stepped into the entry, looked around at the dark rooms, and frowned. "Are you sure you want me here?"

"More than anything." He closed the door and faced her. "I was having trouble being here alone tonight. I'd decided to go on up to bed."

She didn't say anything for a second and he wished he knew what was going through her mind. Finally, she started unbuttoning the long coat she had on. But she held it firmly together and studied him another second.

"I brought you a Christmas present." She clutched the coat together even more. "Well, sort of."

He had one for her, too. Something he'd bought during the wild month between Thanksgiving and moving here. He hadn't planned on giving it to her quite yet. But maybe…

"All I need is you." He stepped toward her, noticed her trembling. "Is something wrong?"

Without a word, she let the coat slip from her shoulders, pool at her feet.

He blinked in shock, before he grinned in pure delight. "Hell of a present, darlin'."

She blushed. "I thought of you when I saw it."

"Thought of me taking it off you, right? Because that's damn sure what I intend to do."

Her eyes darkened and he saw the way her breasts swelled toward him. The way she breathed rapidly. "I'm sorry, Ryan."

Her quiet words were like a punch to the gut. "Honey, you're *not* the one at fault. I'm the idiot who didn't treat you right." She started to speak, but he shook his head. "No. I let time get away from me. Let all of that rodeo craziness keep me from thinking straight."

"But I—"

He put a finger to her mouth, stopping her protest. "Let me be man enough to own up to my failings. I let you down by not calling, by not something…emailing, whatever."

Her eyes watered and he prayed he'd made progress in winning her back. He decided to lighten the moment, hoping he wasn't making another mistake. "I'll let you make it up to me."

To his relief, she smiled. Mischief danced in those beautiful green eyes. She could do anything she wanted with him. He was hers plain and simple.

Krystal's heart raced, her stomach fluttered as if filled with nervous butterflies. This wasn't the first time they'd made love, or the first time she'd been in charge. She'd walked into his house, looked into his love-filled eyes, and known she'd wrongly judged him. He might have a serious flirtatious streak, but when he gave his word about something, he held to it. He hadn't exactly said in so many words that she belonged to him or that he belonged to her.

"We're going to have to work on some things, cowboy. Like your failure to adequately communicate." Would he take this wrong?

He nodded. "You need more than just my physical loving. You need me to say the words, make sure you understand that I mean them." He trailed a finger along the edge of the fur leading to her cleavage.

She trembled, warmth heated low in her body. She felt her nether lips swelling. "Yes. You can't just assume others know what you mean."

His hand slipped lower, shifted inside the babydoll to cup one of her aching breasts. He gave her that crooked oh-so-sinful smile of his. "I get that now. Learned the hard way and nearly lost you." He lightly pinched the nipple. "I'll tell you every day that I love you for the rest of my life."

She moaned, feeling moisture between her legs, and her clit twitched with longing. She glanced down at the thick erection tenting out his jeans. "Talk about *hard*."

"Only for you, darlin'." He put her hand on him and groaned as she gently squeezed. "Think we could take this little reunion upstairs? Before I can't walk."

She giggled. Then she looked up at him and quietly admitted, "Dad wasn't too happy about me coming here tonight. Even threatened to get the brush." She'd known he hadn't meant the threat. His eyes had been worried. He'd been angry, yes, but because he didn't want to see her get hurt again.

Ryan pulled her against him and she felt his thick bulge rubbing at the place so ready for him. He reached around to cup her buttocks. "If you need a spanking, I'll turn you over my knee."

He massaged her cheeks and held her tightly. "There's nothing quite as nice as seeing your sweet ass turn a pretty pink." He rubbed back and forth, torturing her with yearning. "Except maybe seeing those legs of yours spread nice and wide for me."

"If I have a choice, I'll take option two. Legs spread wide. Lying naked and ready for you to find your way home." She reached around him to pinch one taut butt cheek. "You have a great ass, too, cowboy."

In retaliation, he slapped her bottom. "Be nice or I won't give you that ring."

"What ring?" She pushed him back, looked at him with such hope in her gaze.

He heaved a sigh. "Damn. I meant to do this differently, another time."

"What?" she asked breathlessly.

He seemed to weigh something in his mind. Then he blew out a deep breath and scooped her into his arms. He carried her upstairs to his bedroom and set her gently on the side of the bed. "Wait there."

She couldn't have moved if she wanted to. Breathing was all she could handle as she waited impatiently. He went to his dresser and dug around in the top drawer.

He faced her with two things and a hesitant look. One was a two-sided paddle he'd come home with for her on a visit once. One side was leather, the other was fur. They'd played with the fur side several times and her body shivered in memory. Good memories. Very good memories.

He must have noticed her interest and the way she squirmed in longing. With a grin of understanding, he set it on the dresser. "Later, darlin'."

Then he looked uncertain, shifted nervously. After a couple of awkward seconds, he walked toward her with a small box in his hand. His tan had faded a bit. She almost took pity on him, sensing what he was building up the courage to do and hoping she was right.

"I...I..." He cleared his throat, looked unsure how to proceed.

Fighting a smile, she motioned him down.

He took the hint and went to one knee in front of her. He still appeared pale and nervous. But he opened the box and she nearly lost it seeing the gorgeous diamond. She sniffed a couple of times, then tears trickled silently down her face.

"Are you crying?" he asked in disbelief. "Am I doing this all wrong?" He started to stand, grumbling, "Damn. I knew I'd screw this up."

She shoved on his shoulder to keep him from getting to his feet. "You're doing just fine. But hurry it up, please."

He frowned. "Patience, woman. This isn't easy."

She wanted to drop to the floor in front of him, hug him to her. She wanted to kiss him all over, again and again. Instead she sat primly, waiting, holding out her left hand.

He pulled the ring from the box, grabbed her hand, and moved to slide the ring on her finger. She curled her ring finger under. "What?" he asked in confusion.

"Words. That 'failure to communicate' thing we talked about earlier. *I want the words.*" Her heart raced. Was she pushing him too far?

Sinking back to sit on his heel, he sighed. "Right. Words." He met her gaze and slowly smiled. "Will you marry this hard-headed cowboy? Will you spend the rest of your life being patient with me as I mess up from time to time? Will you let me love you?"

She couldn't sit still another second. She slid from the bed and straight into his arms. She was sobbing but she had to kiss him before she took another breath. "You're all I've ever wanted."

He didn't let her kiss him, nudged her back, lifting his hand that still held the ring. "First things first, darlin'. I need the words, too. Yes? No? You'll weigh your options?"

She thrust her hand at him. "Yes." Then she lightly punched him in the stomach. "Weigh my options? Did I have some?"

"Nope, not really." Then he glanced toward the dresser. "We're wasting time here. I've got a sweet ass to paddle. Some legs to spread."

"I'm for skipping ahead to the kissing and legs spreading thing."

He stood, pulled her up, and kissed her. In the next instant, he tossed her on the bed. "Time to peal you out of that little get-up." He waggled his eyebrows. "Then…"

She watched him strip, savoring every wonderful inch of him. *Mine. All mine.* At last.

A Special Gift for Her Cowboy

"Maybe we could get away for a few days? Take a four-day weekend." Christina stepped out of the bathroom with a towel wrapped around her and glanced toward the bed where Joshua was pulling on his work boots. "I'm sure I could get the time off, especially with it being so close to Christmas."

The man she still craved every time she looked at him even after five years of marriage barely glanced at her. Once he would have walked to her with heat in his eyes and torn the towel off her and then… Today he just went back to what he was doing. Her heart sank, feeling pinched and heavy. Her stomach tightened. Tears threatened, as they had been doing a lot lately. She was sick to death of feeling so much frustration. She turned back into the bathroom to finish getting ready for work.

"Can't, darlin', and you know it." He sounded as if he were chastising a child for begging for a new toy. "This has been a crazy month with half my men taking time off to go be with their families for the holiday. I'm needed here more than ever."

Christina leaned against the vanity, bracing her hands and squeezing her eyes shut. Disappointment curled through her. She *wasn't* a child wanting something she didn't really need. She wanted something a woman had every right to desire: time and attention from her husband. She battled down the urge to stomp her foot in anger, to snap back at him in protest.

Instead she swallowed her hurt and said, "I understand."

There had been a time when she'd felt as important to him as his ranch. Over the last few months she'd begun to feel as if she were only another burden for him to bear. The ranch had suffered from the bad economic times like every other business. He'd had to lay off three good men and she knew he struggled to keep the remaining six ranch hands. She'd gone back to being a secretary, a job she'd never liked, but she'd wanted to help out. She didn't resent having to do it, but she missed being a stay-at-home wife and doing more around the ranch.

She knew Joshua didn't like her going off to work every day in Colorado Springs, either. His ego had taken some bruising when it had become necessary. Somewhere along the line he'd stopped being the easy-going, good-humored man she'd married. His smiles were a rare thing anymore. The long hours he'd spent loving her late into the night were not much more than a fond memory now.

"I'll be going into the city this afternoon to get some supplies." He stepped into the doorway, frowned at her as their reflections met in the mirror. "Are you pouting about us not being able to get away?"

She raised her chin. "Not really, but I *am* disappointed." She waited for him to respond to her lie, they both knew she *had* been pouting.

He looked at her for several long seconds, but finally heaved a sigh and backed away. "Life's full of frustrations and sometimes we just have to deal with them."

He didn't even give her a goodbye kiss before he planted his worn Stetson on top of his in-need-of-a-trim blond hair. "I'll be late getting back. I'm meeting some old friends at Pete's Bar tonight."

"You've got time for them…but not me." The bitter words came out before she could stop them. She knew they weren't fair. He worked hard. He worked from before sun-up to long after sundown most of the time. But she missed him.

Still bent over the vanity and looking at him in the mirror, she blinked in surprise as he walked into the bathroom. He shoved the towel up over her bare bottom with one hand and smacked her hard once with his other hand. Then he strode away without another word.

The single swat stung, but she savored it. He hadn't taken the time to warm her bottom in months. Not that she liked getting spanked, but at least when he did spank her, she had his undivided attention for that short amount of time.

In truth, he'd hardly touched her for more than a quick kiss in a good three weeks. She hadn't gotten a kiss this morning either, but at least he'd touched her. She'd have to do some thinking, some planning, but one way or another she was going to get her husband's fully focused attention on her by Christmas, which was only a week away.

* * * *

Joshua jerked his sheepskin coat on and scowled as he went out the back door. A cold wind out of the north hit him square in the face. Small flakes of snow swirled around him. The day promised to be a trial. The snow would make the normal chores a bear. Most days recently had been a trial to get through, but financially things were getting better for the ranch. He was damn glad about that.

He stared out across the ranch yard, knowing he should get moving, but reluctant to do so. He'd swatted his wife's butt and not for a good reason. She'd been disappointed by his refusal to consider taking time away from the ranch to be with her. He knew he'd hurt her further by announcing he would be spending time tonight with some neighboring ranchers instead of with her. No doubt she was frustrated by their not having made love in…in too damn long. *Hell!* What kind of husband had he become lately? She deserved far better than a worn out rancher who came dragging in every night only to eat in a rush so he could go drop into bed. He crashed in exhaustion long before she even came up to join him. *Hell!*

He'd lifted that towel, seen her delectable bare butt, and his dick had gone rock hard. Had he yanked down his jeans and done what his body had wanted? *No.* Idiot man that he was, he'd swatted that creamy skin instead. He liked spanking Christina, liked the feel of her soft skin beneath his calloused hand, and liked watching the flesh turn pink. He also liked flipping her to her stomach and then sinking between those hot cheeks. It had been far too long since he'd given her a spanking—and she'd certainly needed more than a few in the last couple of months. He just hadn't had the energy to deal with disciplining her. Or with making love to her. *Damn ass stupid is what you are. Got your priorities out of whack.*

His foreman spotted him on the porch and nodded in greeting to him. Time to get working. He forced the problems with his wife to the back of his mind. Later, as he drove into town, he'd do some thinking. He'd been dropping the ball in this marriage and it was time to pick it up and get back into the game. Seriously. Christmas was only a week away and he had better find time to shop for his wife. She deserved something nice…but he couldn't manage time away right now.

****

"Can I help you find something?"

Christina nearly jumped out of her skin, her face heated. Warily she looked sideways at the young woman all gothed out complete with heavy black eyeliner, black lipstick, and a black dress that barely covered the essentials and knee-high black boots. She had stopped in the Naughtily Yours store on a whim while on her way home from work. If she hadn't been desperate for a very special Christmas gift for Joshua and if tomorrow wasn't Christmas Eve she never would have dared come in here. But she *was* desperate.

Pulling in a steadying breath, she said, "I need something…" The heat spread higher on her face. "Something special for my husband as a gift."

The salesclerk's lips spread into a knowing smile. "You want to give him something that you'll both enjoy. Maybe something a bit naughty."

"Um, yes." *Forget this. Walk out the door and go home.* Yet her feet refused to obey her thoughts. She had a couple of shirts, some new boots, and a new DVD for Joshua. They were OK gifts, but B.O.R.I.N.G. She wanted a gift that would shock him, that would…

"We've got all kinds of flavored massage and body lotions, vibrators, dildos, anal toys. Any of those interest you?" The slightly younger woman headed toward the other side of the store.

Christina's heart raced. They'd done the flavored lotions and Oh Wow! What her husband could do with his tongue as he lapped chocolate from her body. She had a couple of vibrators stashed in her nightstand drawer, but they hadn't been used in a long, long time. When Joshua was in the mood there was absolutely no need to even think about a substitution for his long, thick cock. And she was determined to get him interested in her again. As for anal toys…No, at least, not now.

She didn't move from the board of hanging items she'd been studying. "Actually, I was considering one of these." Could her face get any redder?

The salesclerk turned around, grinning, and hurried back. "Wanting to play the naughty wife? Always fun."

Focusing on a two-fingered, over a foot long, two-inch wide white tawse with four red hearts, Christina wondered just how "fun" it would be to feel it lashed across her bare bottom. Her stomach fluttered at the idea. Her husband had whacked her a few times over the years with his belt when she'd been really "naughty." The experiences hadn't been close to enjoyable. But she'd learned a memorable lesson each time. Still, did she dare give him something like this?

"These can sting like the very devil." The clerk removed the tawse from a hook and handed it to her. She smiled, her eyes dancing with knowledge. "Applied just right it can be a serious turn-on, for both of you."

It felt firm yet oddly soft in Christina's hand. She ran her fingers over the hearts and felt her panties getting wet. Turned-on is right. But did she really want to give Joshua something that he could eventually use in a far less playful manner?

Before she could change her mind, she nodded. "This will be perfect."

* * * *

He was such a loser of a husband.

Joshua's shoulders slumped as he stood in front of the sparkling Christmas tree and the meager three wrapped gifts he'd gotten for Christina. He'd probably even gotten the wrong sizes, the wrong colors. Gift buying was *not* his thing. Lately even being a decent husband wasn't his thing.

He heard his wife's soft footfalls on the hardwood floor, smelled the scent of the strawberry body lotion she favored. With each step closer, he tensed. He didn't want to face her and see the disappointment on her face when she noticed that he hadn't added any new gifts for her under the tree. She'd added a new gift for him earlier today, something that had made her blush when he'd caught her setting it down. He'd wondered about it ever since. Now he felt like shit for not working harder to get Christina a gift that would really show her how much he loved her.

She walked up behind him and put her hands on his shoulders. He tensed even more; at the same time his dick hardened so much he hurt. "Are we still opening the presents in the morning?" Maybe he could come up with some brilliant plan before then. Go online and get her a gift card for something, or arrange for a trip like she'd been wanting.

Her hands moved slowly down his arms and his muscles tightened at the soft touch. "I've got one I want you to open tonight."

They had always saved the presents for Christmas morning. He panicked, certain she wanted to give him something special. He didn't have anything really special to give her. Filled with regret, he faced her. "I suck at buying gifts."

To his surprise, she smiled and nodded. "I know. But it doesn't matter."

She stepped by him and bent over to pick up the brightly wrapped package she'd put under the tree this afternoon. As she leaned down, the short red silk robe she'd changed into after dinner rode up. He stared at long, shapely legs and that sweet ass he loved, an ass sporting a whisper-small red lace thong. He sucked in a badly needed breath, swallowed hard. Gawd a'mighty, he wanted that ass. Minus the thong. He wanted her less every scrap of clothing beneath that robe and on her hands and knees in the middle of their big bed. He wanted her head lowered, that long brunette hair draping around her slender neck, and that ass up nice and high for him to...

Before he could finish that vision she stood and held out the gift for him to take. He resisted pulling her to him instead, sensing she was eager to give him whatever it was. Her cheeks had turned a pretty pink and she had trouble meeting his gaze.

"I hope you will like it. That you won't think me foolish." She worried her lower lip. Lips he wanted to kiss, a mouth he wanted to plunder.

Curiosity filling him, he ripped the paper off to find a long, narrow box. He looked up at her again and noticed her watching anxiously. Even more curious now, he lifted the lid from the box and gaped in shock. Never in the world would he have expected a gift like this. She didn't like it when he disciplined her, which he hadn't done in too long. But she'd sure been pushing his buttons lately. They'd never done spanking as foreplay. Not that he was against the idea. Hell no. There were few sights he liked better than having Christina's pretty ass over his knee. But it surprised him that she might want some spanking fun.

He lifted the leather tawse from the box and met her eyes. "Oh, darlin', this is one damn fine gift." He shook his head. "I don't have anything nearly as special for you."

She reached out and touched the side of his beard-stubbled face. "The only gift I need from you is *you*."

All he could do was stand there, wishing he were a better man, wishing he had poetic words to give her in return.

She dropped her hand and he noted the hint of disappointment in her eyes. Then she turned and headed out of the great room. "The second part of this gift will be upstairs in the bedroom."

Was she serious? She wanted him to use the tawse? Could he be so lucky? He sure as hell didn't deserve to be. But damn if he was going to pass up this opportunity if she was really offering it.

* * * *

Am I crazy? Can I really do this? Christina walked as calmly as she could manage away from her puzzled husband. Her stomach fluttered with nerves the entire walk up the stairs. Her heart pounded.

"Hands and knees on the bed," Joshua called up to her, sounding huskier than normal.

She froze for a second, tingling all over. If she could actually go through with this, he would smack that leather tawse across her bottom *Oh god, oh god, oh god!* She could stop this. She could change her mind.

You will not *chicken out now.*

"Take off everything but that thong." He still hadn't followed her, but desire laced his words. He liked the thong, the one she'd debated over buying, uncomfortable things that they were. But she'd bought it for him, another gift of sorts.

Her hands shook as she walked into their bedroom and she looked toward the bed they'd shared for over five years. Where they'd once had such wild, uninhibited sex. Where he'd occasionally sat on the edge and turned her over his knee for a spanking. Where he would soon apply that naughty gift to her bottom.

Slowly she moved across the large room and removed her robe, tossing it on a chair near the dresser. Then she took off the short nightie top she'd also recently purchased and added it to the chair.

Pulling in a wary breath, she crawled onto the bed. She moved into a familiar punishment position, leaning over until her forearms hit the thick comforter. Her bottom rose high, making her feel awkward, vulnerable…and excited. This time it wasn't about obedience, about waiting to be disciplined. No, this time she took the position out of love, out of anticipation. Moisture beaded the thong. Her clit ached, pulsed. She wanted Joshua so much.

"You're so beautiful." She hadn't heard him walking up the stairs or entering the bedroom. But she heard the lust, the need in his voice and she shivered.

She craned her head to glance back at him, trembling even more at the obvious heat in his expression and the sight of the tawse in his hand. "My bare bottom is pretty much all you can see. How can that be beautiful?"

His lips lifted into the sinful grin she hadn't seen in far too long.

"Darlin', I love that sweet ass of yours."

Feeling bolder than she had in a while, she wiggled her bottom at him. "What you love is burning my bottom."

He swallowed hard and walked closer, appearing unable to stop staring at his goal. "I don't mind heating up your backside, particularly not when you need it." He met her gaze. "But I don't like hurting you, ever."

She thought about the gazillion times he'd spanked her, sometimes pretty darn hard. Those times had caused her some real discomfort for hours, occasionally a day or so. But never once had he finished disciplining her without holding her close afterward. Her strong-willed husband believed in domestic discipline, but it cost him. He suffered almost as much as she did…almost.

"I know." She nodded toward the tawse, nerves dancing inside her again. "Going to try out your gift?" Then she added quickly, "This is just for—"

He stepped next to the bed, smiled. "For heating things up. Foreplay."

"Yes," she whispered, trusting him as she always did.

His eyes had darkened, his nostrils flared and he gently ran a hand over her buttocks. They quivered in response. He grinned and then fingered the tiny strap of the thong. "I really like this."

She didn't so much, but she'd wear it for him once in a while. "Another gift for you."

"I'm the worst husband ever." Such sadness filled his face that her heart ached for him. "I haven't told you, like I should every damn day, how much I love you. How much I need you."

Tears misted her eyes. "Words aren't always necessary. I know you love me. I love you, too."

He frowned, looking angry. "I haven't *shown* you how much I love you either. I'm always coming home so damn tired. I—"

She wiggled her bottom again, distracting him as she'd hoped. He really was a bare-bottom loving man. "How about we try out your new toy?" She gave him what she hoped was her most sexy smile. "Then you can spend the rest of the night *showing* me how much you love me."

Relief settled over him, the tension left his tight shoulders. "Sounds good to me, darlin'." He gently pushed her head down to touch the comforter. "I'll not abuse this special gift you're giving me. I won't hurt you."

In the next instant the tawse landed across the middle of her buttocks. Lightly, so lightly she barely felt anything. Then another almost equally light slap landed. Not good enough. Not building any kind of fire in her.

"You can do better than that," she grouched, hoping she wasn't pushing him too far.

He chuckled. "My sassy woman wants to feel a sting, huh?"

Maybe she should rethink that. "Just a bit more."

He thwacked her bottom twice, both times a lot harder than before. Hard enough that she arched downward and gasped. But he followed those slaps up with a smoothing of his hand and a pair of cotton-soft lashes. This time she purred and shoved her bottom back.

"I really like this gift, darlin'. But I'm not sure how much longer I can use it. At least not this time." He ran it lightly over her bottom and she shivered. He chuckled once more. "You're so responsive, so sensitive."

"I'm responsive to *you*. Always you." She closed her eyes, wanting him, wanting to please him in every way. He might not like hurting her but he did like seeing her red bottom. Something about it turned him on and she wanted him deliciously wild tonight. Whatever pain he caused her would pass soon enough. "Show me what kind of sting your gift can really deliver. Turn my bottom red."

"I don't know...."

She looked around at him, frowning. "Do you love me or not?"

He stood quietly, seeming to consider her question, her implied demand. As he raised the tawse, she dropped her head again. The thwack this time resonated throughout the room. She cried out and fisted the comforter in her hands. "So that's a *yes*?"

"Damn straight." He gritted the words out and landed two more hard thwacks.

"Ookkkkay!" She screamed. "You love me!" Her bottom blazed where the tawse had landed and she blinked back tears. She'd asked for this, but it would be a while before she did so again.

The bed shifted and her husband's big body stretched out beside her. He pulled her next to him, smoothing his hand down her back, kissing the top of her head. "You've got the prettiest red ass now."

"Happy?" she whispered.

"Happier than I have a right to be." He set the tawse next to him and looked at her with concern in his eyes. "You going to stick with me a while longer? Give me another chance?"

She glanced at the tawse. "I should whack your bottom with that thing for doubting my love for you."

"Not happening. This head of household issue is one-sided. You can go nose-to-nose with me at times, argue until we're both red in the face, but only one of us will ever get their butt burned." He cupped her face. "You, darlin'."

She rolled her eyes. "Pretty unfair."

He shrugged. "Yep."

She was tired of this discussion. It was time to move onto the other things she wanted. "You're wearing too many clothes."

"Can't deny that." He shot from the bed and pulled off his boots and then everything else. He watched her the entire time and she watched him.

She rolled to her back, felt the slight sting when her tender bottom touched the comforter. As she stared at the long, thick cock more than ready for her, she awkwardly tugged off the thong and threw it to the floor. "So Head of Household, going to take charge of your woman in another way?"

The look he gave her was so hot she shivered in anticipation. "Damn right I am."

The End

About the author

Starla Kaye wears many hats professionally and as a writer. She is the community coordinator for a Midwestern accounting firm, a gerontologist who volunteers with an active group of senior adults, a mentor/teacher of writing, and a multi-published author. She dabbles in writing romances of many sub-genres: contemporary, historical Western, medieval, sci-fi, fantasy, paranormal, and Regency. To date she has published 20 novels, 37 novellas, 7 anthologies, and 15 short stories.

Also by Starla Kaye

Holly's Big Bad Santa

Jared had left Danville, Kansas thirteen years ago determined to never look back. He'd hurt too many people and believed he couldn't go home again. He's a much harder man now and at a turning point in his life, filled with uncertainty.

Holly has decided to let go of the past and begin a new life in California. She'd loved Jared most of her life, but she was finally giving up hope of him returning home. Even if he did, neither of them were the same people who'd been in love all those years back. He'd made his decision to leave his family and her behind. She was making hers now. Another man wants her to be with him and she aches to be loved again.

As he is recovering from nearly dying, Jared he receives a message from his parents. They want him to come home for the holidays. And they tell him the young woman he'd once loved is preparing to leave town forever. Right or wrong, he can't continue to stay away. He has to make peace with Holly and with his family.

But is it too late?

Other titles by Starla Kaye

Our Lady Gloriana
Her Cowboy's Way
Rose's Cowboys

Latest titles from Black Velvet Seductions

Right Place, Right Time by Leslie McKelvey
Playing for Keeps by Glenda Horsfall
The Love She Wants by Mila Winters
Holly's Big Bad Santa by Starla Kaye
Punished! by Richard Savage, Nadia Nautalia & Starla Kaye

See more of our titles at
www.blackvelvetseductions.com

Our titles are available from:
Amazon
Smashwords
LuLu
Nook
Blushing Books
All Romance eBooks
Bookstrand
and other retailers